Cruises
Can Be
Murder

Connie Shelton

Books by Connie Shelton

THE CHARLIE PARKER MYSTERY SERIES

Deadly Gamble	*Stardom Can Be Murder*
Vacations Can Be Murder	*Phantoms Can Be Murder*
Partnerships Can Be Murder	*Buried Secrets Can Be Murder*
Small Towns Can Be Murder	*Legends Can Be Murder*
Memories Can Be Murder	*Weddings Can Be Murder*
Honeymoons Can Be Murder	*Alibis Can Be Murder*
Reunions Can Be Murder	*Escapes Can Be Murder*
Competition Can Be Murder	*Sweethearts Can Be Murder*
Balloons Can Be Murder	*Money Can Be Murder*
Obsessions Can Be Murder	*Road Trips Can Be Murder*
Gossip Can Be Murder	*Cruises Can Be Murder*

Holidays Can Be Murder - a Christmas novella

THE SAMANTHA SWEET SERIES

Sweet Masterpiece	*Sweet Payback*
Sweet's Sweets	*Sweet Somethings*
Sweet Holidays	*Sweets Forgotten*
Sweet Hearts	*Spooky Sweet*
Bitter Sweet	*Sticky Sweet*
Sweets Galore	*Sweet Magic*
Sweets, Begorra	*Deadly Sweet Dreams*

The Ghost of Christmas Sweet
Tricky Sweet
Haunted Sweets
Spellbound Sweets - a Halloween novella
The Woodcarver's Secret

THE HEIST LADIES SERIES

Diamonds Aren't Forever
The Trophy Wife Exchange
Movie Mogul Mama
Homeless in Heaven
Show Me the Money

CHILDREN'S BOOKS

Daisy and Maisie and the Great Lizard Hunt
Daisy and Maisie and the Lost Kitten

Cruises
Can Be
Murder

Charlie Parker Mysteries, Book 22

Connie Shelton

Secret Staircase Books

Cruises Can Be Murder
Published by Secret Staircase Books, an imprint of
Columbine Publishing Group, LLC
PO Box 416, Angel Fire, NM 87710

Book layout and design by Secret Staircase Books
Cover images © Elvira Shamilova, Liudmila Holmes, Almoond,
Kshatry
First trade paperback edition: March, 2024
First e-book edition: March, 2024

* * *

Publisher's Cataloging-in-Publication Data

Shelton, Connie
Road Trips Can Be Murder / by Connie Shelton.
p. cm.
ISBN 978-1649141644 (paperback)
ISBN 978-1649141651 (e-book)

1. Charlie Parker (Fictitious character)—Fiction. 2. New
Mexico—Fiction. 3. Private Investigators—Fiction. 4. Women
sleuths—Fiction. I. Title

Charlie Parker Mystery Series : Book 22.
Shelton, Connie, Charlie Parker mysteries.

BISAC : FICTION / Mystery & Detective.

813/.54

For Dan and Daisy, my pack, always.

Chapter 1

The lovely scent of bacon and maple syrup drifted toward me. I stretched in bed and breathed deeply. That lasted about thirty seconds before I decided to hop up and find out what my fabulous husband was working on in the kitchen. I donned a terry cloth robe, quickly brushed my teeth, and headed in that direction. Drake was already dressed in jeans and a fitted t-shirt, his dark hair damp, showing off the touches of gray at the temples.

Not surprisingly, our little brown and white spaniel, Freckles, was sitting at his feet as he flipped another pancake on the griddle. Her eyes never left Drake's hands, even when he stepped back and bestowed me with a kiss.

"What's your plan for the day?" I asked as I took the plate he handed me and set it on the kitchen table.

"A photo shoot for a music video," he said, sitting and reaching for the pitcher of warm syrup. "The cinematographer and director are meeting me at the hangar at nine. We'll be up near Shiprock for an hour or two. Total flight time should be about four. What's your day looking like?"

"Just the office. I've got a few invoices to send out to clients, mostly Ron's standard employment background checks, I suppose. We haven't had any terribly exciting investigations in the last month or so." I glanced down at the floor, where Freckles had conveniently shifted her furry little bottom over and positioned herself to stare at our plates. "I'm sure once the food is gone, she'll be eager to come along with me."

I caught him sneaking a bit of pancake down to our little beggar. "If I finish early enough in the day, I was thinking of coming home and cleaning up the gazebo. It's almost warm enough to enjoy some evenings outside. It would be fun to invite Gram and Dottie over for a cookout, maybe."

"This weekend might work for that." He was studying the weather app on his phone, checking the forecast.

"I hate to disturb them too early, but I can pop over there later in the day." I carried my empty plate to the sink and ran hot water over the sticky residue, then made my way toward the shower and clean pair of jeans that were waiting for me.

Twenty minutes later, he'd changed into his flight suit and we headed out to our vehicles. Drake left for the Double Eagle Airport, while Freckles jumped into the back seat of my Jeep, eager to begin her routine day at RJP Investigations. Our offices are in a gray and white Victorian, which sits under a huge sycamore and an old cottonwood, which were just leafing out with fresh spring green. Albuquerque had made it through the winter with little snow this year, and I was looking forward to warmer weather and more outdoor time. In the parking area out back sat Sally's minivan and Ron's Mustang. I pulled in beside my brother's car.

Sally Bertrand, our part-time receptionist with the outdoorsy style and purposely disheveled blonde haircut, was in the kitchen when Freckles and I walked in through the back door. Already the coffee maker was sputtering to produce its first carafe full. Sally has worked with us almost as long as we've been in business. We've attended her wedding and seen the birth of her kids. I tend to lose track, but I'm pretty sure they're both in school now.

"Hey, Charlie," she said, stretching to set the coffee canister onto a shelf. "Ron said to tell you there's a new client coming in this morning. Talbot Farber."

"The car sales guy?"

"Owner of, like, half the dealerships in the state, I think."

I knew the Farber name. Farber Auto, a real Albuquerque success story.

The coffee maker finished doing its thing, Freckles begged a dog cookie from Sally, and we all headed toward the front of the office. While Sally settled in at her desk, I climbed to the second floor, where my office sat across from Ron's. After sticking my head in to say hello, I crossed into mine and set down my bag and booted up my computer.

"I think you should sit in on this morning's meeting," my brother called out. "It's Talbot—"

"Farber. Yeah, Sally told me. Do we know what he wants to hire us for?"

"No clue. He just left a message saying he wanted a meeting. Sally confirmed the appointment time. Guess we'll find out."

"Maybe he wants you to start doing all the background checks for his business. There'd be quite a few, I imagine." I picked up my mug again and walked over to his doorway.

"I get the feeling it's something else," he said. "But he wasn't very specific. I've been doing a little research on the company history. Seems like he started out with one mid-sized dealership selling cars made in Detroit and has picked up so many more, his interests now include high-dollar autos from Europe and Asia, both gas and electric models."

"Must be doing well."

"Victoria and I went to a party at some horse ranch out on Rio Grande around the holidays. She pointed out the Farber place. It's—woo. Huge."

"I guess we'll learn more when he gets—" The bell on the front door chimed downstairs and I heard Sally greet someone. "—here."

Sally buzzed Ron's office on the intercom and, downstairs, I could hear her ushering the client into the conference room, offering coffee. My brother looked up from his desk, piles of manila folders and takeout containers stacked precariously around his computer. "Okay, ready."

Ron stood up from his desk, flicking potato chip crumbs from his shirt and giving a nod toward the downstairs conference room. He smoothed back what remains of his hair, and straightened his shoulders. I headed down the stairs ahead of him.

A tall, distinguished man in an impeccable dark suit stood in our conference room, his salt-and-pepper hair neatly combed. He had a confident smile that didn't quite reach his eyes. He was better looking in person than from the television ads he used to do.

"Mr. Farber," I held out my hand. His grip was firmer than I expected.

"Please, call me Talbot." His voice was smooth and polished. "You must be Charlotte Parker." He'd done at least a bit of research on our firm.

"Call me Charlie. Thanks for coming in. Please have a seat."

Talbot settled into one of the worn leather chairs, checking out the details of our restored Victorian. Ron walked in, introduced himself and took his normal seat at the head of the table.

"Now, how can we help you today?" he asked, while I grabbed my notebook.

Talbot cleared his throat. "It's about my late wife, Jenna. Thirteen years ago, the two of us went on a Caribbean cruise and—" his voice broke a little "—Jenna vanished. Legally, she was declared dead a few years ago. Kiley and I—that's our daughter—we've managed okay."

"I'm so sorry."

"It's been difficult. For both of us."

Ron was giving the man the eagle eye, trying to figure out what our small private investigation firm could do for him. After about a minute, he came right out and asked.

Farber cleared his throat and straightened in his chair. "I saw Jenna. In Denver, a few weeks back. I swear it was her."

He set a faded photograph on the table. "This is my wife."

The photo showed a beautiful smiling redhead on a tropical beach.

Ron raised an eyebrow. "And she just happened to

pose for a picture?"

"No, no." Talbot chuckled. "This is from our honeymoon." He touched the photo with his fingertips. "But in Denver, I swear it was her. Same eyes, same smile."

I leaned forward. "Did you speak to her?"

"Well, no. I didn't get the chance." Talbot slid a few handwritten letters across the desk. "These are in her handwriting. You'll have them for comparison, if you want."

Ron examined the letters, frowning. I met his eyes briefly. Was it a typical case of a supposedly dead spouse turning up years later? With those cases we'd heard of, most of them never turned out to be a real sighting, normally just a case of mistaken identity combined with desperate hope. On the other hand, we couldn't rule out anything at this point.

I pulled my notebook closer. "Why don't you start from the beginning? Which cruise line and what was the date?"

Talbot nodded, his eyes distant as he recited the information. "As I mentioned, it was thirteen years ago ..." He took a deep breath before continuing. "Jenna and I were on a Caribbean cruise for our fifth anniversary. We were having a great time, enjoying the sun, the food, the entertainment. Then on the third night, I woke up alone in our cabin."

His voice turned hollow, haunted by the memory.

"She was just ... gone. No note, no signs of struggle. Her clothes and luggage were still there. The crew searched the ship but it was as if she had vanished into thin air. I just never imagined I'd be returning from the cruise alone." He stared up at the ceiling, blinking rapidly.

I pictured it—the panic rising as Talbot realized his wife was missing, the fruitless searching of the ship. A chill went down my spine. I found myself scribbling notes. Ron typed away at his laptop, already starting the background research.

I turned to the client. "But you saw her recently?" I prompted.

"Yes, at the Denver airport!" His face lit up. "I was there on business. I was grabbing a bite at a pub on the concourse when I saw a woman across the way. She had the same auburn hair, the same slender build. And although she turned toward me for only a brief moment, I swear it was Jenna's face."

"But you didn't get the chance to talk to her?"

He shook his head sadly. "No, by the time I picked up my briefcase and shuffled through the tables and got out into the open, she was way ahead. There was a flight a few gates away that was boarding for Albuquerque. I think she got on it, but the gate personnel wouldn't tell me a thing, and they wouldn't let me walk onto the plane to look for her."

"You were on a different flight, going somewhere else?" Ron asked.

Talbot nodded. "I was on my way to an important meeting in Chicago."

I paused, weighing how to respond. False sightings of dead loved ones weren't uncommon. But something in Talbot's voice gave me pause. I could tell Ron was interested in taking the case.

"We'll look into it," I said finally. "If she's out there, we'll do our best to find her."

Farber signed our standard contract and paid a retainer for two weeks' worth of our time.

As we saw him out the door and watched him get into a gleaming Rolls Royce, Ron and I exchanged a look. On his part, I saw car-envy in his eyes. As for me, I wondered what we were getting ourselves into.

Chapter 2

Ron holed up in his office while I checked in with Drake. His job was going well. The singer and his band had showed up on time for the video shoot (not always a sure thing, in his business), and they'd done flights over the surrounding red rock formations that would set the tone for the storyline, the cinematographer getting some amazing shots, he said. He promised to text me when they were ready to head back to Albuquerque.

From Ron's office I heard the incessant clicking of computer keys and knew he wouldn't want to be interrupted, so I went back to my regular duties. Ron is the licensed private investigator here and I'm the accountant for the business. However, being such a small firm, I'm often pulled into the investigations in more ways than planned. And sometimes that's fine. I love getting out and about, and it'd been a long winter stuck at home. If I got assigned to dash up to Denver and check out what Jenna Farber was doing there, that was fine with me.

Meanwhile, I caught up my bookkeeping entries, prepared billing statements for our regular clients, and carried the envelopes downstairs to Sally's desk. Yes, some of them still insist on getting things through the mail. Sally would drop them off when she left for the day around one o'clock. She also assured me Farber's check would be deposited on her way home.

It wasn't quite noon when Ron called out from his mancave-office. I could hear his printer whirring in the background. "Anyone up for lunch at Pedro's?"

Anyone meant me, and of course the answer was yes. I'm always up for my favorite green chile chicken enchiladas.

"Soon as I print these reports," he said.

Freckles lifted her head from the puffy bed near the window seat in my office. Now that she's not quite such a puppy, she lounges around most of the day, although when anyone comes in the front door she's down the stairs and racing to greet them. Our regulars know her as a staff member and a few even bring treats in their pockets. Strangers get a good sniffing, but our little spaniel knows to leave them alone. It occurred to me that she hadn't even approached Talbot Farber this morning. What did that say about him?

I heard Ron's squeaky chair roll across his chair mat, so I cleared my desk and gathered my purse. And even though Pedro and Concha are quite willing to let Freckles join us near our usual table, this time I bribed the dog with a treat to remain in her crate at the office.

We each took our own vehicles. I didn't know whether Drake might need me to run out to the airport, and Ron had plans to meet Victoria this afternoon to choose a new sofa. He followed me toward Old Town and we each fended for ourselves when it came to the limited parking along the street near Pedro's restaurant.

I walked inside first and gave a nod to Pedro, who was carrying a basket of chips to another table. Ron greeted him heartily and told him we'd each have our usual, minus the margaritas, which I'd learned from experience were better saved for later in the day.

Once we were settled at our table with chips and salsa before us, Ron pulled a background form from the folder he'd carried inside.

"You may know a lot of this already," he said, "since the Farber empire has been established in New Mexico a long time."

We'd all observed the progress as Talbot's father began in the 1970s as a young businessman with a single car dealership, one of the big Detroit brands. Once his son joined him, the family enterprises began to multiply like rabbits. They now claimed more than two dozen dealerships, all over the state, representing domestic and foreign makes and models. We had his home address in the lush part of the north valley, where some prestigious horse ranches had begun to crop up; no home phone, but the personal cell number was one he'd given us during our meeting.

A second sheet was a credit report, which seemed in keeping with the man's obvious lifestyle. Kiley was in private school, and had graduated early, head of her class at the end of the last semester. She'd already been accepted to an Ivy League school next fall.

Our lunches arrived, delivered by Pedro's wife, Concha, who set the plates down and then draped her arm around my shoulders for a hug. We did a one-minute catch-up before she instructed us to eat while the food was hot. I didn't have to be told twice.

As I cut into the steaming concoction of corn tortilla wrapped around tender chicken, with melted cheese, sour cream, and Hatch green chile sauce that'll knock your socks off, Ron told me he'd found several news stories dating back to the tragedy aboard the *Queen of the Caribbean*.

"You can read the whole story—I'll send you a link, but basically it says there was a fire aboard the ship. It was a small one, but people panicked, apparently. Several went overboard. All were rescued except Jenna. Her body was never found."

"Wait a minute. Talbot made it sound like she vanished from their cabin in the middle of the night. He said nothing about a fire and other people going into the water. What the hell?"

"I know. The original article only said that one female passenger was never accounted for."

"Okay, and they must have had a way to know which passenger was missing, and the cruise line knew who it was. They surely notified whatever authorities."

"This all happened off the coast of Belize, and they did notify the coast guard and police there. A later article names Jenna Farber as the missing woman."

I felt my brows furrow as I set my fork down. "Was her husband considered a suspect? I mean, people fall off cruise ships and there's usually more to it."

"Eventually they ruled it a disappearance at sea. They seemed to think it was a tragic accident or possibly a suicide. None of the articles refer to Talbot as a suspect, but I've sent requests for copies of the reports with the local police and the cruise line. They'll include more detail than what was released to the media."

Ron leaned back in his chair, frowning. "I gotta be honest, finding Jenna Farber seems like a long shot. It was thirteen years ago, and the cops investigated pretty thoroughly."

"I know, I know," I said. "But didn't you think it was strange they never found a body?"

Ron shrugged. "Could've been taken by currents. Or eaten by sharks."

I shuddered at the thought. "Still, if there's even a chance she could be alive ..."

"But she never checked in, not in all this time?" Ron raised an eyebrow. "Why would she do that? They had a young daughter."

"I don't know," I admitted. "Amnesia, maybe? Money, another man ... there could be reasons."

Ron sighed, running a hand over his bald spot like he always did when he was thinking. "All right, sis. I know that look. You've already made up your mind that we're going to pursue it."

I smiled. "We accepted Talbot's money. We at least have to give it a shot."

Ron rolled his eyes but couldn't hide a grin. "Fine. But when this turns out to be a dead end, a case of the client mistaking someone else for his wife in Denver, you're buying the margaritas."

"Deal." We shook on it. I was already making a mental list of where to start digging on this cold case.

We finished our lunches and said goodbye to Pedro and Concha. Outside, Ron handed me the slender case file he had started. "We still need the actual police reports, witness statements, etcetera. The newspaper clippings are just a start. Good luck. I gotta go buy a couch, but this evening I'll get on the phone and see about calling in some favors."

"Ron—do you believe Talbot? I find it really suspicious that he failed to mention there was a fire aboard the ship."

Ron pulled out his phone, hit a stored number, and tapped the speaker button when Talbot answered. Not one to mince words, he put the question directly to our client.

"I didn't? Are you sure? The fire was—yeah, it was kind of a big deal, for about a minute. Alarms went off all over the ship and we were told to go to our lifeboat stations, the whole bit. It didn't take them long to figure out it was really a small fire near one of the kitchens, and it was quickly put out. I got back to our cabin and realized Jenna wasn't there, so I reported her missing after waiting thirty or forty minutes. It wasn't until later in the morning I heard several people had gone overboard and were rescued."

Okay, that was slightly different from his first version of the story, but all I could do was file it mentally away. Ron thanked him for the clarification and hung up.

"You think it's possible she jumped?" Ron asked as we walked toward our cars.

"I don't know," I admitted. "The fact that others went into the water too, and there was a fire on board. I can see where people would panic. But something feels unfinished. Even if it turns out to be true—that she died in the ocean and it was someone else Talbot saw in Denver—maybe we can give him some peace of mind."

Ron grunted, whether in agreement or skepticism I couldn't tell. I watched him climb into his Mustang and drive away. Without any further word from Drake, my best bet was to go back to the office and continue with the case.

Thirty minutes later, I was typing away on the computer, searching databases for any records on Jenna Farber, nee

Caldwell. Marriage, divorce, criminal—anything we could get.

I read the articles in the file that Ron had summarized, refreshing my memory on the details. As Talbot had told us, there were no signs of a struggle or foul play. The working theory with the local police was she had fallen or jumped overboard in the confusion.

According to a profile I found in *Vogue*, Jenna had been a 28-year-old model and aspiring actress when she met Talbot Farber. It was a fairytale romance, with a beautiful wedding. They were married just at the point when his business had taken off and turned him into a billionaire. They had one child, a girl. From that, and the other accounts, they seemed happy enough.

Wait a minute—billionaire? I stared at the page. I knew car dealerships were lucrative, and I could see a family becoming multi-millionaires by that means. But billionaire is a jump way beyond that. It was another thing for me to file away and check on later.

For now, I debated Talbot's idea that we should go to Denver and find out which flight Jenna was on, the day he spotted her. That was really a long shot, and probably a complete waste of time. Airlines were notoriously close-mouthed about their passenger manifests, and I didn't have the law enforcement credentials to break open their records.

I put a call in to Kent Taylor, Ron's detective buddy at APD. I've worked with him before, sometimes on shaky terms, but we've recently developed a sort of mutual respect. Kent is a homicide investigator, but I was hoping he knew someone who could help me.

Chapter 3

By the next morning I still hadn't heard anything back from Kent Taylor. Drake would be busy most of the day at the airport. His helicopter was due for a hundred-hour inspection and he would be cleaning the equipment after the mechanics smeared their greasy little paws all over it. Freckles (with clean paws) was with me in my office, giving me the cute-doggie stare, in hopes that I would cross the room and get her a treat from the cookie jar on my bookshelf.

I ignored her as I squinted against the morning sun glaring through my south-facing bay window. Ron had sat hunched over his desk all morning, scrolling through files on his computer. I gave up on the sludgy coffee in my mug and was headed downstairs as the front door opened.

"Good morning," said Talbot Farber, striding in. Once

again, he exuded success in his neatly pressed steel gray suit, sharp white shirt, charcoal tie, and salt and pepper hair.

"Morning." I studied Talbot's confident smile. Yesterday, he'd brought us a troubling case, yet this morning he looked unbothered.

"I'm checking on the progress with my case," Talbot said.

"Well, it's only been one day. We're in the process of contacting the airlines at the Denver airport, to see if she was on any passenger manifests, and I believe Ron is working to see if we can get some surveillance footage." I didn't admit to him that it took police assistance to get those things, and we hadn't yet made any progress there.

I hesitated. "Talbot, have you considered that it might not have been Jenna you saw?"

He crossed his arms. "It was her. I know my own wife."

I took a deep breath. Even though his pushy demeanor bothered me, I thought of his teenage daughter, Kiley, who probably barely remembered her mother. If Jenna was out there, the girl deserved answers.

"We'll find the truth, Mr. Farber," I said firmly. Talbot nodded, his eyes showing a glimmer of hope.

"Let me know the minute you learn anything. Anything at all," he said. This time, his tone was a lot more subdued. He shook my hand and sent a little salute toward Sally.

As he left, Ron came down the stairs, carrying the handwritten letters our client had delivered yesterday. I headed to the kitchen at the back of the old building, where I saw that Sally had started some fresh coffee.

Ron rubbed his chin as he handed me the letters. "Better keep these in a safe place until we have something to compare them to."

I paced the kitchen, thinking aloud. "Just playing devil's advocate here … how could Jenna just reappear after all these years? Why now?"

"Beats me." Ron reached for his favorite mug. "We need more to go on. Until we get access to airline records, I say we start getting background info on Jenna, leading up to her disappearance. Who was she before she met and married Talbot? That kind of thing."

"Good idea. We could interview her former co-workers, friends, anyone who might remember something." I held out my mug so he could pour for me too.

Back upstairs, I grabbed my laptop to start making a list. Thirteen years ago, social media was hardly a thing, but I figured it was worth a try, to see if Jenna's name came up anywhere. If her own accounts had gone inactive, maybe friends would have mentioned her. It didn't take long to find myself buried in the quagmire of posts, finding that I couldn't go nearly far enough back in time.

Turning to the old *Vogue* article again, I pulled a few clues. Jenna Caldwell had been raised in Los Angeles, was a popular fashion model (not exactly super-model status) by the time she was twenty, and met her husband while living and working in New York. That bit of information gave me at least two leads. The modeling agency had been acquired by a larger one about five years ago, and I dialed that number.

"You're looking to hire one of our models?" asked the person who answered after I'd somehow tapped the right extension to get a human on the line. It wasn't immediately clear if this was a male or female I was speaking with.

"Actually, I'm inquiring about a model who worked for the agency in the past, probably about twenty years ago."

"Oh, honey, I'm afraid you're out of luck on that. When the merger happened, we purged all records more than six years old. If a model hasn't been active in the past two years, frankly, his or her career is in the tank anyway."

Sad. But I thanked them anyway.

My next idea was to see if I could find any of Jenna's hometown contacts, on the remote chance that she'd stayed in touch with old friends who might shed more light on her state of mind than her husband was willing to share with us. I'd gotten the distinct impression that we were getting a glossy version of the happiness level in the Farber home.

Los Angeles and the surrounding area feels dauntingly big, but it can be small-town in surprising ways. Using the name of the city and one of those "find your high school friends" apps, I learned that Jenna Caldwell attended one of the public high schools in Pasadena.

From there, I got images of a yearbook and discovered Jenna was active in drama club, French club, and sang in the chorus. And there in several pictures she stood next to a girl named Stacy Chavez. Stacy, bless her, had remained in her home neighborhood and was now a proud mom, posting pictures of her own daughter and the volleyball team. I sent a message, asking if she remembered Jenna and got an immediate reply.

Absolutely remember Jenna! What are you up to, girl!!

Obviously, Stacy had got the message mixed up and thought I was actually Jenna. For the moment, I could go with that.

Would love to talk—call me! Followed by my cell number.

My phone rang thirty seconds later. Then, of course, I had to do a little backtracking, explaining who I was and why it was important for me to know if Jenna had been in touch with any of her old friends, especially in the last thirteen years.

Stacy was initially a bit surprised, but oddly not wary of me. I would have been, had someone called me with such an outlandish story. She said they'd lost touch after Jenn's wedding. Rather than jealousy, I sensed pride in her voice. She rattled off several more names of classmates and I scribbled as fast as I could to catch them.

"Would you mind asking around? Quietly, of course. If anybody has seen or talked to Jenna since she married, I'd love to talk with them. She may be in the Denver area— that's where her husband saw her recently."

"Absolutely. I see two of our closest friends every week at our daughters' volleyball practice. I'll put the word out."

"If anyone knows anything, please give them my number."

She promised. I didn't hold high hopes.

While I was busy cultivating Jenna's old friendships, Detective Kent Taylor had left me a voicemail to say he'd found a way to request airline records on our behalf. He would email me the results.

My thoughts kept drifting back to Kiley. The poor girl had grown up without a mother, and that situation hit really close to home for me. By now, Kiley was nearly the same age I'd been when I lost my parents. So, if Jenna was out there somewhere, I wanted the daughter to know. She deserved a chance at a relationship with her mom. That is, assuming Jenna wanted it too.

I felt a renewed determination to unravel the mystery, and the truth—elusive as it was—pulled at me.

* * *

Freckles and I arrived at home a little before five, and Drake pulled in shortly after, bringing takeout from his favorite chicken place. I still felt a bit stuffed from my lunch at Pedro's, but I did manage to help myself to a couple of wings and a portion of the side salad. I filled him in on my day.

"Wish I had something to offer," he said, "but all I know about Farber is that I bought a truck from one of the dealerships. That's been a bunch of years ago."

"You don't happen to remember any news stories about the disappearance of his wife, huh?"

"Don't forget, I was living in Hawaii until I met you. So, no." He dumped the chicken bones in the trash and gave Freckles a generous chunk of biscuit. "But you know who you should ask? Elsa. She may be ninety-ish, but she's got a mind like a steel trap."

"And she's lived in Albuquerque her whole life."

My husband is such a smart guy. I picked up a borrowed plate that Gram had sent home with me, filled with cookies two days ago, and I went out the back door and stepped through the break in the hedge between our houses.

In the light of Gram's kitchen window I could see Dottie Flowers, her caregiver, working at the sink. I tapped at the back door and then let myself in. Gram was sitting at the table, dumping out a box of dominoes for their nightly after-supper game. I set the plate down, apologizing that I was returning it empty. I hadn't baked anything in weeks.

"No problem," Dottie said. "You wanna join us for Mexican Train?"

"I need to get back, but I have a question for you, based on a new case Ron and I got this week."

Dottie dried her hands and set the kettle on a burner.

"Do either of you remember the story about a woman named Jenna Farber, who vanished from a cruise ship some time ago?"

"Farber. That's the car dealership guy, right?" Elsa asked as she slowly shuffled the dominoes in wide circles.

"Right. He's the one who hired us." I gave them the basics of what we'd been told. "I vaguely remember the story being in the papers here. Local woman vanished, devastated husband returning home without her …"

"Oh, yeah …" Dottie said, pointing an index finger upward, as though that helped bring the vision back. "She was like some real pretty little thing. She'd been a model or somethin' and the news cameras kept hanging around their place …"

"Showing that poor man and their little girl. He seemed so broken up about it," Gram added. "How come he's hired you now?"

"That's where it gets interesting. He thinks his wife is still alive."

"Ohmygosh, yes. Her body was never found," Dottie exclaimed. "I'm rememberin' it now."

"Yes, that's the one." I turned to each of them. "What else do you remember about it?"

Gram, with an index finger on one domino, twirling it in place, gazed upward. "Thinking about the husband now, I remember when he used to do his own ads for the car places. You know, there was something about him I just didn't like."

"In what way?"

"Something in his eyes. Like he was trying *too* hard, wanting everyone to believe he was very successful and at the same time he cared more about what car was best for your needs, like taking your money meant nothing to him. It was all about making you happy with your car." She abandoned the domino and clasped her hands on the table. "But down inside, I could always tell it was about the money. For him, it was about being Albuquerque's most successful businessman."

"Yeah! Yeah, *that* was it," Dottie added. "I thought it too. And when them news people were pestering him about his wife ... oh yeah, I saw some flashes of anger. It was like 'how dare you question me.' He was sendin' that message."

"Interesting." I'd come over looking for clues to the case itself and received, instead, a couple of wise women's insights into our client's personality. And I had to admit I wasn't surprised by what they'd said.

I excused myself, saying I'd let them get on with their evening game. When I walked back through the hedge and opened the back door, Freckles greeted me as if I'd been gone a week.

"Silly girl." I gave her a tickle behind the ears. And then a cookie.

Drake was in our home office, filling out his logbook for the day's flights. I picked up my phone and scrolled through emails, pleased to see one from an Alan Woodson, detective with APD. This was Kent's contact guy, but unfortunately all his message said was that he'd been tied up on a case for several days and hadn't had time to get me the information I needed on the airline records. I was mulling over that information when my phone rang—a number I didn't recognize.

"Is this Charlie Parker?" The voice was female, maybe about my age. "I was given your number by Stacy Chavez, a friend of Jenna Caldwell's."

"Yes! I'm glad Stacy gave you my number. What did you say your name is?"

"Sorry—I'm Barb Walker. I saw Stacy at our kids' gym this afternoon. She said you're asking about Jenna?"

"Yeah, actually wondering if you're still in touch with her."

There was a sigh. "No, sadly, I haven't heard anything from Jenna since shortly after her marriage. Gosh, it has to be seventeen, eighteen years ago now. We were best friends in high school, but then life took us in different directions."

"In what ways?" I heated water and brewed a cup of tea, settling in for what might just be a lot of reminiscing that had nothing to do with my quest. But I'd see what came of it.

"Jenna was always a dreamer," Barb said. "But she was the kind whose dreams turned into firm plans. From the age of twelve, she'd decided she wanted to be a super model. And what do you know—she developed into a beautiful young woman and went off to New York. I'm not sure she ever made it to the top ranks, you know, but she was always in demand."

"I'd heard she was a model ..."

"Oh gosh, she had so many dreams. She would sit on my bed, polishing her toenails when she spent the night, and tell the rest of us how she would be married to a really rich man, and they would live on an island whenever she wasn't off in Paris for the big fashion shows. She had a way with clothes, taking something simple and accessorizing it, parading across my room as if it were the runway." Barb chuckled at the memories.

"You stayed in California all this time? Did you ever

meet her husband, Talbot Farber?"

"Oh yeah. When she brought him home to meet her folks. I think it was soon after they met in New York. Her dad was older than most of our parents, and they still lived in Pasadena. Talbot's success in business was pretty impressive. I remember that. I think Jenna told me she'd met him in New York, but he was from somewhere out west, Albuquerque, maybe?

"Anyway, their wedding was here. Pasadena. Jenna chose me as her maid of honor, and Stacy, Ellie, and Kristin were bridesmaids. What a fun summer that was, all of us getting wrapped up in the wedding plans. We kept in touch by phone for a while afterward, then it was Christmas messages, and eventually just lost touch. Probably because the rest of us went away to various colleges, then we began to have our own families."

I'd carried my tea to the living room and settled into a corner of the sofa. "Did any of your other friends stay in touch with Jenna after that?"

"Not that I know of. Once she moved to New Mexico with Talbot, her life seemed to be all about him. She gave up modeling, which was kind of sad, since she'd really wanted that for herself."

Since Barb hadn't mentioned it, I broached the tough subject. "Were you aware that she disappeared off a cruise ship thirteen years ago?"

"No! Ohmygosh, *no*. I never heard that."

So the media coverage hadn't extended much beyond local? I hadn't been aware of that. I filled her in on the basic details, how Jenna had been presumed lost at sea, and told her about Talbot hiring us because he was now convinced Jenna was still alive.

"Wow. I don't know what to say. Do you think it's true?"

"We're just getting started with the investigation. So far, we have no evidence that she is. But if you or any of your friends should happen to hear from her, please—"

"Oh, absolutely. I just can't stand thinking about our beautiful Jenna being gone forever."

I nodded, even though she wouldn't know that. "Both of her parents have passed on, right?"

"Yes. Her dad died about a year after Jenna's wedding, I think. Her mom lived long enough to know Jenna had a little girl—I do remember Mrs. Caldwell telling me that. But she also passed away, maybe a year or so after that." Her voice broke, a little. "It's just so sad for that family. I wonder whatever happened to that little girl, with her mommy gone."

I planned on finding out.

Chapter 4

By the time I ended the call, Drake had wandered into the living room wearing nothing but a low-hanging pair of pajama pants, flashing me that smile of his. He settled on the sofa next to me, gathered me into his arms and, well, one thing led to another. I quickly forgot about the case when he took my hand and led me to our bedroom.

As I drifted toward sleep later, something about the phone call this evening tried to work its way to the surface, but my body was too caught up in a mellow afterglow to remember what it was. I turned out the lamp and snuggled up to my husband's body.

A whimper was the next sound I heard, and I opened my eyes to see light around the edge of the drapes and a wistful dog beside the bed. Freckles was giving me her standard morning greeting, which meant 'take me out and then feed me.'

I pulled on a robe and followed her to the back door. While she circled the yard and did her business, I started the coffee maker and scooped nuggets into her bowl. With the dog back inside and hungrily wolfing down her breakfast, I showered and dried my hair before returning to pour my first coffee of the day.

Meanwhile, Drake had warmed up last night's biscuits and magically somehow produced gravy. I suspected a packet of some kind, but that was fine. It tasted great. We shared our plans for the day as we ate, then each went off to our own work. I arrived at our RJP offices to find Sally at her desk and Ron on the phone.

Sally handed me the latest mail, and I walked upstairs while she gave Freckles a treat from her own secret stash. Before I'd offloaded my purse and jacket, Ron hung up his phone.

"What's new?" he called out from across the hall.

I walked into his office and filled him in on the email that had yielded no results regarding flights between Denver and Albuquerque. Then I told him about Jenna's friends I'd spoken with and the fact that our missing woman seemed to have lost touch with her former crowd long before the cruise ship disaster.

He pointed to his phone. "None of my cop buddies have seen or heard about any Jenna sightings here in town."

I leaned back in the chair, perplexed. "So it doesn't seem that she just showed up here out of the blue. Talbot must be mistaken."

"Or dreaming. Or lying," Ron said.

I thought for a moment. "Let's think about that. What would be his motive?"

Ron shrugged. "Money issues? Kid problems? Who knows what skeletons he's got rattling around."

"We need to dig deeper into Talbot's background," I said. "Finances, relationships, anything fishy."

Ron nodded. "I can run a full background check on him. Might turn up something useful."

I glanced at the old photo of Jenna again, feeling sad for her yet more determined than ever to uncover the truth. She actually could be out there somewhere. Maybe? We knew so little at this point.

"I'd like to talk to Kiley, the daughter," I told Ron.

"Good idea."

"I can't imagine that she's curled up, mourning the mother she would barely remember, but she must have feelings about this. Especially if Talbot has told her he spotted Jenna recently."

"Do you think he would do that?"

"No idea. Some kids might be able to handle that news. Most would probably be a wreck, once they really thought about it. I just need to talk with her and see if I can gauge her attitude about the whole situation."

One thing that had been bothering me ever since Talbot walked in our door was this: If Jenna had survived her fall into the sea, why hadn't she reached out to her young daughter in all these years? It was another reason I had doubts about Talbot's sighting of his wife. But I needed to know.

After calling ahead to let Talbot know I wanted to speak with his daughter, I got the address from our file and headed out, letting Freckles ride along. It was a cool spring day, decent enough for her to wait in my Jeep with the windows partway down. We took Rio Grande Boulevard north, where properties went from modest homes on average lots, growing to two- and three-story homes on acreage, to downright ostentatious mansions. White board fences enclosed some of them, with horses grazing contentedly on the spring-green grass.

I took a deep breath as I pulled up to the Farber's sprawling mansion, a Spanish style two-story, stuccoed pale tan, with a red tile roof and lengthy walkways leading to a gazebo on the north and a pool house to the south. Well-established ivy grew up the walls, and weeping willows added grace to the front of the property.

What must it be like for Kiley, growing up in a place like this? I imagined her friends coming here as a kid for pool parties and sleepovers. So much must have changed since Jenna disappeared.

As I walked up the winding flagstone path to the front door, I noticed two gardeners at work on the property, setting out bedding plants in tastefully arranged groupings. How large a staff did Talbot keep, I wondered.

I rang the ornate doorbell and a moment later, Talbot himself answered. As always, he was dressed impeccably in a tailored suit.

"Charlie, good to see you again." He ushered me inside the grand foyer. "Kiley's up in her room, and I've told her you were coming."

I nodded, glancing around. Glazed Saltillo tile floors stretched ahead, where I glimpsed wide glass doors to the backyard and pool. To the right was a living room the size of my entire house, and on the left a dining room held a table that must easily seat twenty. I had a flash vision of some movie in which two people sat at opposite ends of such a monster, never speaking to each other. The whole place felt cold and hollow somehow.

Talbot glanced at his watch. "I've got to leave for a meeting in fifteen minutes."

So, now I knew my time limit. As I climbed the curved staircase, I heard faint music coming from Kiley's room. I took a deep breath and knocked softly.

"Come in," she said in a monotone voice.

I opened the door and got my first impression of the poor little rich girl. Curled up on her bed in sweats, she looked so small and fragile. Her long blonde hair was pulled back in a messy bun and her eyes were puffy. The pout on her face and the earbuds told me she was tuning out the world.

"Hey Kiley," I said gently. "I guess your dad told you why I'm here? Just wanted to check on you."

She sniffled and yanked out the earbuds. "Why bother? Dad says even when she was here, she wasn't really much of a mom."

I sat on the edge of the bed. "Is that how you remember her?"

"Actually, I barely remember her at all." She nodded toward a framed photo on her nightstand. "That picture's really about it."

"But you still have your dad, and your grandparents."

Kiley scoffed. "Yeah, right. All he cares about is his money and his reputation."

"Surely that's not tr—" I started, but she cut me off.

"Okay, Grandma and Grandad Farber have been good to me." She picked up a small pillow and jammed it behind her back. "Dad ... well ..."

She glanced toward the door, which was standing open. When she spoke again, she'd lowered her voice even further. "Dad's there for me. Always."

I put a hand on her shoulder. "Look, I don't have a lot of time to chat today. I guess your dad told you he thought he saw your mom, from a distance, in Denver."

She nodded.

"I need to ask—have you seen her? Either recently or in the past? Has she ever come up to you in a public place, called you, or maybe sent you something in the mail?"

She shook her head. "Nothing. Grandma used to talk about how sweet and pretty Mom was. She told me how much my mom loved me. I just want that back. I'd give anything to see her again." Her voice cracked and her eyes welled up.

"I know," I said. "Ron and I are doing everything we can to find out what happened to her. We won't stop until we figure this out."

Kiley managed a faint smile. "Promise?"

I squeezed her hand and swallowed hard. What would I have given, at her age, for someone to bring my own parents back to me? "I don't know how this will go, but I promise to figure it out."

I squeezed Kiley's hand once again and stood up, sending her the most reassuring look I could muster. Her pain was a palpable thing. I swallowed back my own memories of lost parents as I traversed the upstairs hall and walked down the carpeted stairs.

At the bottom stood Talbot, looking upward as if he'd been waiting for me. Perhaps he had.

"Charlie. I'll walk you out. I was just leaving for my meeting."

I thanked him and came up with a compliment about the house. He beamed a bit, and I got the feeling if there'd been more time he would have showed me around, to impress me with his success. We stepped out to the wide, covered portal and then took the path to where I'd left my Jeep. I noticed a dark SUV in front of the garages, one that had not been there when I arrived.

"How did your conversation go with Kiley?"

"Fine. The idea that her mother may be nearby has affected her. Are you sure it was a good idea to tell her, before we were sure Jenna's still alive?"

"What did she say?"

I debated whether to claim client confidentiality, but that doesn't actually exist for private investigators, not the same as for lawyers or doctors. Plus, I had a feeling Farber would call my bluff. He was no dummy. "Just that she'd love to see her mother again," I told him.

"So she hasn't. Jenna hasn't been in touch with Kiley?"

"She said no. She's heard nothing."

"Did she say anything about me?"

Again, fishing for information. I gritted my teeth. "Just that you've always been there for her." It was absolutely the truth, although I put a somewhat different tone on the comment than what I'd gotten from Kiley. "Why? Did you think she would say something else?"

His mouth went to a straight line for a moment but he realized it and gave me a smile. "Not at all. Kiley and I have always been close."

"Really? She talked mostly about her grandparents, very fondly. I got the impression you were so tied up with your business ventures that she was mostly raised by them."

Talbot's expression darkened.

I backtracked and softened my tone. "Talbot, you came to us. You spotted someone you believe to be Jenna and we were hired to find her. Plus, I made a promise to help Kiley, and I intend to keep it." I met his glare steadily. "She deserves the truth, Talbot."

He turned, averting his stare, rubbing a hand across his smooth jaw. "You're right. She does. I guess I just expected it to be a little easier and quicker than this."

"We're doing the best we can, Talbot, but these things can really take time. Be patient. We'll keep you posted."

I got into my Jeep without another word, my mind swirling. Freckles stared out the side window and growled from the back seat. Talbot was hiding something; I was sure of it. And I would find out what it was.

As I steered down the long driveway and made the left-hand turn onto Rio Grande, his black SUV was right behind me. Kiley's voice came back to me, the part where she said her dad was right there—always—and I hadn't gotten a good feeling. Was this what she felt like?

Despite Talbot's flash of impatience, I felt energized. The mystery of Jenna's disappearance had plagued this family for over a decade, and now that we might finally be on the cusp of unraveling the truth, he was getting bossy. The man was an enigma—he wanted Jenna found, but I also had a strong feeling he was hiding something. He seemed to love wielding power, and the other day he'd made no secret of the fact that he had friends in high places.

Once his vehicle left my rearview mirror at the on-ramp to I-40, I headed back to my office, mulling over the sparse facts we had. Thirteen years ago, had it been an accident? Suicide? Murder? If Talbot had something to do with it, he most certainly wouldn't have hired us to poke around.

And if Jenna was still alive, as Talbot claimed, where

had she been all these years? Why would she abandon her daughter? None of it made sense. Again, I felt a pang for Kiley. She deserved to know what really happened to her mother.

I tightened my hands on the steering wheel, bristling over Talbot's abrupt tone. No matter how much attitude he exhibited, I would get to the bottom of this. As the old cliché went—the truth was out there somewhere.

I'd just pulled into the parking area behind the Victorian, angling in between Sally's minivan and Ron's Mustang, when my phone rang. Kent Taylor, the detective.

"Charlie? Um, sorry for the call. I meant to let you know you're getting a text."

"Hi, Kent. What's up?"

"Ron's had me pulling strings since yesterday. Says you guys need access to some old airline passenger manifests. So I called a guy who called a guy. And because it's beyond any statute of limitations we could find, we got it."

"That's great. You were going to text me all this?"

"Actually, no. Since your request isn't relating to any of my homicide cases, I reached out to a detective in Major Crimes. His name's Alan Woodson, and he'll be texting you a link to an internal server at the FAA, and a code you'll need to log in. Your access is limited to searching flights more than ten years old, so don't get too cocky about it."

"Me? Kent, really, would I?"

"I'm not going to answer that." He comes across gruff, but there's a teddy bear in there somewhere—I think.

I dropped my teasing tone. "What I meant to say was, thank you so much. You really did pull some strings to get to the Federal level."

"Yeah, well it was more than one guy calling one other

guy—there's a lot of favors being called in on this one."

"Can I ask why? I mean, you may have more serious things to use your favor quota for."

His voice went lower. "Truthfully and off the record ... I can't stand Talbot Farber, so I hope you can prove the s.o.b. wrong."

"Dare I ask why?"

"Why I can't stand him ... because he refused to warrantee what was absolutely a lemon of a car I bought once. Why I want to prove him wrong about this newest thing about his wife ... not sure. But I'd hate to see the poor lady back under his thumb."

Okay. I had no response to all that, so I thanked him again for his assistance. Pocketing my phone, I let Freckles out of the car and watched while she circled the perimeter of the yard before we went into the office.

My phone pinged with Detective Woodson's incoming text as I passed Sally on her way out. It must already be early afternoon. How the time flies.

"Ron's upstairs," she told me. "Based on the groans and flying swear words, I don't think it's going all that well."

Chapter 5

For a guy who spends half his life on a computer, Ron reaches a frustration level fairly fast. Apparently things had not gone well today, I discovered when I tentatively poked my head around the doorframe to his office.

"What's up?" I really tried to make it sound sympathetic.

"Damn search engine has crashed on me twice." Ron stood and stretched, staring toward the ceiling. "I'm just impatient with it."

I leaned against the door and filled him in on my visit to the Farber home, including my impressions of Kiley's fragile state and Talbot's quick flash of anger when I questioned him.

"What did you learn in your background search?" I asked.

"The Farbers have lived in Albuquerque a long time.

Talbot has parents who are still here and a brother, Graham, who went to school back east and then took a job in London." He flopped back into his chair and reached for a notebook page of scribbles. Just then his computer screen came back to life. "Ah, this is better than trying to decipher my writing. I can just forward you the links to the articles I've found."

"That's okay. Give me the condensed version." If I'd wanted to read everything on the internet about the Farber family, I could have done the research myself. But I didn't say so.

"Okay, here goes. When Talbot and Jenna were first married, they made the society pages as one of Albuquerque's young power couples. Picture 'Thirty Under Thirty' at the local level. He, the heir to the auto franchises, who comes in with big plans for expansion. She, the gorgeous model, with a big heart for charity work. All the usual blah-blah that comes from publicists for those who want their name in the news."

"Sounds like what we've already guessed at."

"Right. For a couple years, that's all there was. Then they had Kiley and the glow was all about what an ideal little family they were. Always photographed at the big charity events, posing with the state's political heavyweights ... on and on."

"A little *too* squeaky clean?"

"Maybe. That's my impression. But with marketing expertise and having your *people* to control what makes the news ... anyone can come across with the image they want to project."

"So true." Freckles dashed past me and put her paws on Ron's lap. He handed her a treat without blinking an eye.

"And it's my job to find the dirt, those things people don't want made public."

"We're not trying to catch Talbot at anything. He's our client. But he has presented us with a mystery to solve …"

"… and if Jenna really is alive and well somewhere …"

"Yeah. We need to know why she didn't come back right after surviving her fall into the ocean. It could have been the heart-wrenching, feel-good story of the decade for the two of them. From what I gather about Talbot, he would have relished that."

"So, he truly believed she had died, and he made the most of his grieving widower state."

I nodded. "There's sympathetic press in those kinds of things too."

Ron clicked another link. "But he's hiding something. I discovered that he'd filed the paperwork to run for political office—governor. This was the year before the cruise. He was at the height of his popularity and probably could have swept the race."

I felt my forehead wrinkle. "I don't remember this at all."

"He very quickly withdrew, almost before his signature was dry on the forms. I had to really probe to find his name."

"Because …?"

"My guess? Because he's hiding a secret of some kind. Campaign managers are expert at digging out dirt on their candidates, and they'll coach the person to either reveal the skeletons in the closet early on and rush to get it out of the voters' minds, or they'll advise getting out of the race. Those kinds of things *will* come out, especially if the election is hotly contested. And in Talbot's case, he was up against the most popular governor we'd ever had. Her people would have dug deep to get rid of him."

A grin formed on my face. "So, what was the secret?"

He shrugged. "No idea. Like I said, he dropped out so quickly hardly anyone ever realized he'd intended to run."

"So, as long as a person is giving to charity, sponsoring good deeds, and has a beautiful wife at his side, no one's going to inquire too deeply into his past. But the political arena is a whole different thing."

"Exactly. Now—" he held up both hands "—I don't know what the reason really was. This is a guess on my part. But I don't trust that anyone is completely, squeaky clean."

"Kent Taylor sure doesn't like him. Felt he got screwed over on a business deal."

"See? Enough of those and a guy's reputation spreads."

"My impression, seeing him in his home and meeting his daughter, is that there's a lot of surface politeness to the man. But your guess that there are deeper secrets … Yeah, I'm not surprised." I stood straight and let out a deep breath. "Well. Woodson sent me links to old airline records. Let's see if I can find some way Jenna might have gotten away and come back here a lot earlier than Talbot realized."

"Meanwhile, I'll see if I can call in a few more favors at APD and see if there's anything on Farber's business or maybe some little criminal infraction that went unnoticed by the media. I tell you, the man cannot be as perfect as he seems."

I'd no sooner plopped down in my chair than Freckles flew past me and down the stairs. I heard the little bell on the door a half-second later. I descended to the foyer to find a tall man bent over and patting our little greeter on the head.

"She's a friendly one, isn't she?" he asked, rising to send a pleasant smile toward me. "I'm Alan Woodson, by the way." At a bit over six feet tall, slender, in his early forties, with a head of thick sandy brown hair, he was the physical opposite of Kent Taylor. Like most of the detectives I'd met, he wore slacks and a jacket. No tie. The jacket probably concealed his service weapon, if I had to guess.

"Oh, Detective Woodson. We didn't know you were coming by."

"Well, I wasn't, necessarily, but then I happened to be a couple blocks from here. I wanted to be sure you received the FAA database link I sent and that it worked okay for you."

"Truthfully, I'm just now sitting down to start working with it."

He nodded. "Taylor told me this was about the missing wife of Talbot Farber. Interesting." A flicker of something crossed his face, but he was good at concealing his thoughts.

"That's true," I said. "I'm just hoping I can find Jenna Farber listed on one of the airlines' manifests."

"You may find the database a little frustrating," he warned. "I've only had occasion to use it a time or two. It's … well, you know, government. Don't expect a slick website, easily navigated. But stay patient. The information is there if you dig."

"Is it okay if I reach out, if I have problems logging on?"

"Tell you what, if you want to do it right now, I can at least make sure you're able to get online with it and that the passcode I sent you is workable."

Wow, a helpful cop. I think I got a little flustered because I waved him right up to my office and let him sit down at my computer. And sure enough, within a few seconds, there was the website he'd sent. He gave me a quick tutorial on how to get around, with a couple of tips and tricks for when the pages didn't respond logically.

"You'll do fine on your own now," he said, turning to give Freckles one last pat on the head as he went downstairs.

* * *

By five o'clock, the glare of the laptop screen was making my eyes burn. I'd been at this for hours now, scrolling through page after page of flight records from the month Jenna disappeared. I'd assumed there would be some basic search capabilities, such as looking for a particular passenger name, but no. Woodson was right about it not being the easiest site to work with. All I could go by were dates and airline names. This database was forcing me to go through flight after flight.

I'd started with the date Jenna went missing, then branched out day by day, week by week. Allowing for the possibility that she'd been injured or had amnesia, I went further—one month from the disaster, two months, three.

Now, I was ready for a back rub and a stiff drink.

Ron stood in my office doorway. "Find anything yet?"

"*Nada*," I sighed. "No flights from Belize to Albuquerque that month under the name Jenna Farber. On a whim, I even searched the names of several of her friends from high school, thinking maybe she'd figured out a way to travel under a different name. How, I don't know, since she would have needed a passport to board a US bound flight in a foreign country. I have to assume Talbot had her passport, since he said all her belongings were left in their cabin."

Ron frowned. "Well, there goes that theory."

My shoulders slumped. I was sure we'd find evidence Jenna returned to Albuquerque after vanishing from that cruise ship. But so far, all our leads had gone cold.

I stood up to stretch my stiff limbs. "I'm going to call it a night. We'll regroup in the morning when we're fresh." But for now, I was spent.

Ron nodded, but I could tell from his furrowed brow that his mind was still puzzling over the case. I knew that look well—he'd worn it almost constantly since we took on the search for Jenna.

I grabbed my bag and keys and headed for the door. Outside, the early evening air was cool and still. The last of the sunlight had turned the face of the Sandia mountains a deep peachy-purple color. And somewhere out there, I hoped, were the answers we needed to finally solve this mystery.

* * *

Lights were on all over our neighborhood when I pulled into the driveway at home and let Freckles out of the car. Inside, I caught a whiff of pizza and hoped it meant Drake had stopped at Papa Murphy's and got my favorite bake-at-home, the Chicken-Bacon-Artichoke.

He was at the kitchen counter, opening a bottle of wine when I walked in and wrapped my arms around him and leaned my cheek against his back.

"How was your day?" I asked, hoping his had been more productive than mine.

"I actually got a tour flight today, some folks from

Idaho who wanted to take a look around our end of the Rockies." He turned to me and kissed the tip of my nose. "I took them right over our little cabin on the back side. The place looks lonely. We should go up there sometime, now that winter's over."

"Definitely. I'll have to figure out when I'll have a free day."

"Still wrapped up with that Farber case?"

"Yeah, and we're not getting anywhere by scouring old records."

The oven timer dinged. Drake grabbed potholders while I pulled out two wine glasses and poured from the new bottle. Once we'd settled at the table, he took up the conversation again.

"So, let me guess. If searching old records isn't getting you anywhere, you're thinking of going there—to wherever Mrs. Farber disappeared."

I gave a rueful nod. "Actually, that's exactly what was on my mind as I drove home. We've got a pretty good idea of where the ship was when the passengers went overboard. It's off the coast of Belize. I want to study the maps and see if I can figure out which direction Jenna might have drifted. If she made it to some shoreline alive, maybe someone will remember that."

"I'd certainly remember it if a soggy person came washing up on a shore near me."

"Right? And especially if she had amnesia and needed help. There could be a whole community who knows the answer."

"But still, how and why would she get from someplace in the Caribbean to the airport in Denver? Maybe she eventually recovered her memory and knew she should come back to Albuquerque?"

"One step at a time, hon. I'll be lucky to find someone who remembers her from thirteen years ago, and then I'll have to see where the next move takes me."

"Sounds like you're going."

I tilted my head and gave a sigh. "Probably."

"Hey all expenses are on the client, right? And Talbot Farber can certainly afford for you to take a little tropical holiday."

"Ha. Ha. Don't know if he'll see it that way, but yeah— why not?" I felt a grin forming on my face.

"Change of subject," he said. "We'd talked about inviting Elsa and Dottie over for lunch under the gazebo. Maybe this weekend? Unless you're gone then."

"Let's play it by ear. I haven't said anything to them yet, but I'd better find out how soon I can get a flight to Belize."

He raised his wine glass and clinked it to mine. "Yeah, you're definitely going."

* * *

After we'd stored the leftover pizza slices and taken Freckles on a short walk through the neighborhood, Drake got out some aviation maps that covered the western Caribbean. From his collection of invaluable paper junk, he also came up with a nautical chart of the area, one which shows the prevailing currents and patterns. We spread them on the dining table and he gave me a quick briefing on how to read them.

"Take these with you. If you can find out the ship's exact location at the time Jenna went overboard, you can probably figure out which direction she would have drifted. Check with the local coast guard to see if any boat captains reported picking up someone from the sea."

"Wouldn't something like that have been reported in the local news? Ron was pretty thorough in his online searches."

Drake shrugged. "You never know."

I was beginning to see how daunting a task this would be, so I started a list of ideas for people to meet with and locations to scout. First would be the offices of the cruise line, where I hoped I wouldn't need to get pushy to find out the ship's location on that fateful night.

By bedtime I'd started a stack of things to take, including the maps and some weather-appropriate clothing based on what my handy weather app said to expect in Belize City for the coming week. I also checked online for flights, then gave Ron a quick call since he and I had barely touched on the idea of one of us going there in person.

My brother is one of those guys who, when presented with something that wasn't his own idea, has a default reaction to resist it. But once we reviewed what we had and hadn't learned from our research here at home, he agreed that my going there wasn't a bad idea. I asked if he'd rather do it himself, and his negative answer didn't surprise me. My brother doesn't care for most things tropical—mai tais excepted—and he seemed more than happy to send me to do the legwork. He agreed to work on lining me up with a guide who would meet me at the airport in Belize.

I went back to my online search, grabbed a ticket for tomorrow morning that would take me through Dallas and get me into Belize City by early afternoon, local time. I forwarded my itinerary to Ron. Now I just needed to wake up pre-dawn and get myself to the airport.

Not surprisingly, my sleep was filled with way too many thoughts and plans. Aside from the fact that Jenna had seemingly vanished into thin air on that cruise—there was no body, no evidence of suicide or foul play—I had to wonder what had happened.

By three a.m. I gave up on the pretense of sleep and opted to stoke myself with caffeine until I boarded that six o'clock flight. I stuffed the last of my clothes into a suitcase. Poor Drake, awake from all of my tossing and turning, offered to drive me to the airport.

"It'll save on parking," was his reasoning.

In truth, I think he just wanted to see me safely past the check-in desk. We kissed goodbye at the security checkpoint. I clutched my laptop bag with its valuable stash of maps and notes, and set off on my adventure.

Chapter 6

The sun blazed down as I stepped off the plane and descended the portable stairs to the tarmac at the Belize City airport. Palm fronds rattled in the breeze. The midday air felt thick and humid to me, pressing in on me from all sides, reminding me of the many times I'd flown in and out of Kauai and the adjustment to the tropical air. I wiped a bead of sweat from my brow and headed toward the small terminal.

During the flight, I'd studied the charts Drake sent with me, but truthfully I didn't understand much about the ocean, the tides, and patterns of the currents. Hopefully, the man who was meeting me here would be a pro at this. Ron had texted me his name: Herbert Jones.

I stood in line for passport control, made it through with no problem, retrieved my one suitcase, and emerged into the arrivals hall. And there stood a white-haired man, wearing white cotton pants, a dark blue Polo-style shirt, a battered black and white captain's hat, and holding a sign with my name on it. I must have brightened when I spotted that, because he stepped forward.

"Miss Parker? Herbert Jones at your service." His accent was delightfully British, reminding me that Belize had been British Honduras until sometime in the 1970s.

He took the handle of my bag and I fell into step beside him.

"I've been studying my charts for the area your brother described to me," Jones said. "He tells me you're looking into the case of that woman who fell from the *Queen of the Caribbean*. Quite the tragedy. Many of us were out in our boats, assisting in the search."

"You remember the incident, Mr. Jones?"

"Herbert, please. Oh, quite well. I never heard that the poor woman was ever found."

"Did Ron tell you how we came to be on the case, why we're searching for her all these years later?"

"No details. Just that there was reason to believe she somehow survived."

"We aren't sure but we have several working theories, no real evidence yet. I'm hoping to find out the exact location where she went overboard and then see if we can figure out, if the currents pulled her or if a boat picked her up, where she might have come ashore."

His blue eyes twinkled. "I believe I can help. Ever since I heard from Ron Parker last night, I've been puzzling over this."

I had subconsciously been heading toward the terminal's exit doors, but Herbert touched my elbow and gave a nod in the other direction.

"We'll most likely be traveling on to Ambergris, but I'd like to show you my charts and my reasoning for that conclusion. Shall we settle at a table in the restaurant—for refreshments and a little meeting?"

"Lunch would be great—I'm buying." Actually, Talbot was buying. "Lead the way."

We settled at a table and ordered sandwiches, then Herbert brought out a navigational chart of his own. Within two seconds he had it spread out and was pointing at a small red dot in the blue ocean.

"This is exactly where *Queen of the Caribbean* was positioned when the fire broke out on board and ten passengers went overboard. Of course, she was traveling slowly, only twelve knots at the time, and the captain brought her to an immediate halt. They were able to rescue all but the one woman."

"That's much closer to land than I'd imagined."

"Aye. Only about two kilometers off shore." He noticed my puzzled expression. "About one and a quarter miles."

"A person in good shape might be able to swim that far."

"Aye, easily. And in this case, with the tide coming in at that hour, the current would have taken them directly towards Ambergris." He traced the path with a finger and jabbed the island he was talking about.

Our sandwiches arrived, but now I was distracted.

"Did no one figure this out at the time?"

"Oh, of course. Once the word got out to the experienced sea captains in the area, we concentrated our search there."

"But no one spotted Jenna Farber?"

He shook his head sadly. "It's a big sea. And it happened in the dark of the night. Apparently the lass had no life jacket with a little beacon light and no other way to signal us. By morning, she would have either landed ashore or been taken by—" Rather than finish the thought, he picked up his sandwich and took a large bite.

I picked at my fries, dipping them in the sauce that had come with the plate. What he'd told me so far confirmed one of my more hopeful theories—that the ship had been close enough to shore that a strong swimmer might have made it to land. Even unconscious, the tide might have carried her ashore somewhere along here.

I still wondered if Jenna could have met up with a waiting small boat. The fact that none of the locals had reported picking her up would take the investigation in a whole new direction, the idea that she might have somehow arranged for someone to meet her, or convinced a local captain not to reveal that she was safe. I didn't voice those suppositions aloud, but I wasn't ruling out anything yet.

"I was hoping that coming here in person and talking to someone in the cruise line offices would be helpful," I told Herbert.

"Good luck with that," he said with a half smile. "The minute the word 'lawsuit' was bandied about, they became a blank slate."

I should have figured as much. Besides, I probably already had the information they might have provided. Ron had done an excellent job in locating Herbert.

"So, on to Ambergris?" I suggested. My conversation with Jenna's friend the other day kept replaying in my head. One of Jenna's big dreams was to live on an island. Could it be that she'd laid low and stayed here all along?

I'd finished maybe half of my lunch, but Herbert had a hearty appetite and had devoured his. He gave a nod.

"We'll take the inter-island flight. It's quick. And once we're there, I know some people I can introduce you to."

I wanted to assure him that he really didn't have to give up any more of his time, but he genuinely seemed to be getting into this. Maybe there's not much else for a retired sea captain to do in a little community like this.

We walked through the terminal to the desk for Maya Island Air, where it seemed my host had already been one step ahead of me. Two tickets were being held in his name; all I had to do was present a credit card. The flight was leaving in fifteen minutes. I gave Herbert a more perceptive look. This old guy was proving to be a valuable asset to our investigation.

We walked directly to the small plane and boarded. Twenty minutes later I found myself staring out at the calm, blue-green sea below, trying to picture how Jenna had ended up in the water that night. Had she been pushed overboard by someone, fallen over accidentally, and what was her condition? Had she been drinking, or half asleep? I wished I could talk to someone who'd actually been aboard that ship, other than Talbot. I was beginning to believe the man had fed us exactly the story he wanted us to hear.

* * *

The sun was sinking lower in the sky when our plane landed at San Pedro Town, where I discovered most of the vehicles were golf carts and the streets primarily made of hard-packed sand. Herbert took my suitcase and led the way to a four-seat cart in the parking area. The key was in it, and this didn't seem to concern him in the least. He placed my case in the back seat and we climbed aboard.

"I'm not stealing it," he explained. "My friend owns a rooming house here and I'd already asked if she had a room for you for the night."

I eyed him sideways, a grin growing. "You've thought of everything."

"Your brother said you'd be tired when you arrived. I'm only doing what any gentleman would."

I turned and gave him a seated, half-bow. "I'm grateful and flattered."

And, I had to admit, getting up at three a.m. at home meant I'd already put in a very long day. I sat back, paying attention as he made a series of turns down cart-sized roads, passing bars, restaurants, and touristy gift shops. Several large condominium complexes sat back from the road, with ocean-facing rooms behind gated walls. But the overall feeling was casual and a lot more low-key than other tourist destinations I'd visited.

A few minutes later, Herbert pulled to a stop outside a private home. The house was built of concrete block painted vivid purple, with a bougainvillea-covered wall circling the property. Two stately queen palms flanked the walkway, and a pair of small, fluffy white dogs ran out to greet us.

"Hello, chaps," Herbert said, reaching to touch their heads when they jumped and placed their paws on his leg. He handed each of them a small doggie treat. "Where's your mum now?"

One of the dogs yipped and both raced toward the front door.

"Looks like guests get the friendly treatment," I said

with a laugh.

"Aye, little buggers know I usually have biscuits in me pockets."

The screen door opened and the dogs raced inside. A lovely black woman stepped out. She wore a loose dress and had her hair up in a twist, with threads of gray running through it.

"Tomasina, this is your guest, Charlie Parker," Herbert said, turning back to get my suitcase from the cart.

"Charlie, welcome." Her voice was like music, part Caribbean lilt with a distinct British accent behind it. "I've got you in the Blue room. Come on through. Are you hungry?"

I thanked her and assured her we'd had a late lunch.

"I always make a pot of something for the evening. Those who are hungry can eat, but there's no pressure. Many like to sample the local restaurants too."

I made a sound that hopefully left my options open. As the late afternoon light dimmed, I found myself thinking only of sleep, but I didn't want to waste Herbert's time. He probably needed to get back to his own home, wherever that might be.

Tomasina led the way past a small parlor and down a short hallway, where several closed doors branched off. She opened one, revealing a bathroom with a large walk-in shower that looked heavenly to me right now.

"This bath is shared with the guests in Green and Yellow," she informed me, "except we have no one booked in those rooms for the next few nights. So, for now, it's all yours."

My super detective powers told me this meant most tourists opted for the larger, fancier condos, while maybe her place was used either by semi-locals or people on business, such as I was. The Blue room was spacious and cool, with blue walls (who'd have guessed!) and a canopy bed dressed in white. Watercolors of island life decorated the walls. Herbert set my bag next to the dresser and I set my laptop case beside it.

"If you'd like a nap or shower, feel free. Supper will be ready in another hour if you're hungry," Tomasina said, stepping out of the room.

I turned toward Herbert, who stood beside her. "I'm not sure what your arrangement was with our office," I said. "You've already been immensely helpful and I don't expect you to give up any more of your time."

"I'm here to be of service, if you wish."

"So you live here on Ambergris, too?"

"No, Belize City, actually." A quick smile and wink passed between the two of them.

"Oh." *Oh!* I blushed furiously. "I'm sorry—I didn't mean to assume anything."

Tomasina chuckled out loud. "Herbie always keeps me company when he's here on the island."

I stammered my way through trying to sound like this was no surprise to me. They saw right through my embarrassment and assured me not to worry. They stepped out and closed my bedroom door. I flopped onto the bed, staring up at the canopy.

I should be making a list of places to go and people to interview, but I have to say, that mattress was like a cloud. I barely got a text out to Drake and Ron, letting them know I'd arrived safely, thanking Ron for my new tour guide, when I fell utterly and completely asleep.

When I woke up, the sky was a pale azure. At some

point I must have kicked off my shoes and pulled the duvet over me (heaven forbid if Herbert had needed to come in here and tuck me in—I wasn't even going to contemplate that). My travel clothes were rumpled from serving as sleepwear, and my hair must be a total fright.

A few minutes in the bathroom with my cosmetic bag and a change to light cotton slacks and a V-neck tee after my shower really helped. I followed the scent of coffee and located the kitchen, where Herbert sat at the table and Tomasina was flipping French toast on a griddle.

She handed me a mug and set a plate of the heavenly smelling toast on the table for me.

"Best tuck in while it's hot," Herbert advised, spearing another chunk from his own plate.

I didn't have to be told twice. Tomasina brought her own plate and sat next to him. I decided they looked like an established couple and wondered how long he'd been making Ambergris and this rooming house his port of call.

"So, what's the plan for today?" he asked as he swabbed the last of the syrup from his plate.

I told him I'd not really made a list of places to visit, but would appreciate it if either of them could steer me toward people who had lived here or been in business during the time Jenna may have come ashore.

"Obviously, if she'd just dragged herself out of the surf and a crowd gathered, a lot of people would remember. But I'm guessing that didn't happen."

Tomasina shook her head sadly. "No. I would have heard. This house would likely be where locals would direct a stranger in need."

As Herbert had directed me here. "You don't remember seeing or hearing anything about her?"

"It's not to say she was never here," Tomasina added. "A lady like that, used to fine accommodations and such. She might have gone directly to the posh resorts at the end of the island."

"Good thinking. I'll check that."

Herbert cleared his throat and pushed his chair back. "I must get back to Belize City today, I'm afraid. Do you have an extra copy of that photo, the one of Miss Jenna? I'll ask around the docks, talk to the sailors I know in the city."

I went back to my room and gathered the maps and another copy of the photo. Back at the table, we cleared space and spread the nautical chart out again, taking another look at the possible spots where Jenna would have been most likely to have made landfall.

"There are a number of atolls and tiny cayes scattered about," Herbert commented, pointing to several little islands, "but the trajectory from the ship to the nearest land would put her here on Ambergris. If by chance she missed that, the natural drift would land her on the mainland, in the middle of nowhere. It's a mile or so of swampy hiking to get to a road or town. Then again, if some kindly boater gave her a ride, anywhere along the coast is a possibility."

I began to see how tricky this might be. But I had to give it my best shot.

"Thank you for offering to ask around. RJP will pay you for your time," I said. "Our client can afford it."

The elderly captain gave me a wink. "It's already taken care of. Your brother covered the tickets, your room, and a little extra for me. Electronic transfers are a new miracle to me, but it works. If costs add up, I'll let him know. For the most part, I'm having the time of my life, helping out."

He left the charts with me, handed me a card for the little air charter company that had brought me here with instruction to call them when I was ready to leave, and then he picked up a duffle bag. Tomasina walked him out, placing her hand affectionately on his shoulder.

When she came back, we refreshed our coffee mugs and she gave me a few names to start with, those locals who'd been here the longest. A bait shop on the docks, a popular bar, and a gift shop.

"A gift shop?"

"Sorry, I realize no survivor of the sea is likely to go shopping for shells and t-shirts," Tomasina said with a laugh. "But go there. You want to talk to Maria Tenorio. She lives right above the shop, and the location has been all sorts of businesses over the years—coffee house, bookstore, fruit market … When one fails, she just opens another in its place. I have no idea what she had there thirteen years ago, but if it looked appealing your lady might have walked in."

I thanked her for breakfast, grabbed a sun hat and my purse, and set out, following the sketch she'd drawn on the back of an envelope—hoping this whole thing wasn't a complete waste of time.

Chapter 7

First stop on my map was the bait shop about two blocks away, where Tomasina had told me a guy known only as Tubb had sold fuel and fishing supplies since she was a little girl. Old Tubb had passed away but his son had worked the shop since he was a kid. Young Tubb was a good source for local gossip, she assured me.

A fresh breeze came off the water, cutting the humidity I'd felt yesterday. I passed a row of small homes before I spotted a few ramshackle places that housed businesses.

I made my way down a rickety dock to the small bait shop perched on weathered stilts at the end. Pushing open the screen door, I stepped inside. The place smelled like the stinkiest dead thing imaginable. I pictured decades of various fish bait passing through these doors, and I nearly turned and ran. A man in his fifties glanced up from behind

the counter, his dark eyes peering out from under a faded
ball cap. He wore a wrinkled blue t-shirt with a scene of
dolphins leaping and smiling.

"Hello there. Are you Tubb?" I asked.

I got a nod in return. The stench didn't faze this guy a
bit. It was probably so ingrained in his pores that he didn't
know it existed.

I walked past a display stand of fishing poles, two
racks of lures, and a bin full of assorted rubber boots and
flipflops. "Tomasina suggested I talk with you."

The man studied me for a moment, then nodded.
"Sure, lady."

I introduced myself and handed over one of my RJP
Investigations business cards, then explained my mission.
As I showed him a photo of Jenna, his gaze turned distant.

"Lots of American tourists come through here. Not
many of them as pretty as this one."

"She probably looked kind of rough at the time," I
suggested. "She'd been in the sea for a few hours. I doubt
she'd have come in to buy anything, more likely to ask for
help."

He handed the photo back. "Sorry, no."

I wasn't terribly surprised. Knowing Jenna's background,
this didn't seem like the kind of place she'd gravitate to.
But it had been worth asking, since the shop was right on
the water. I thanked him and walked out, eager for a breath
of fresh air, hoping the breeze would carry the bait-shop
scent from my clothes.

I left the dock and headed back toward town, checking
my little map again and noting the couple of turns I needed
to make, to find my way to Angus's Place. Tomasina had
told me the popular bar had been so-named since the

1960s, and not to expect to meet anyone named Angus. The current owner was Angus's grandson, Peter Weston.

Peter wasn't on duty when I arrived, but a waitress said he would return any minute. I ordered a Coke and parked myself on a stool near the end of the wooden bar. The place faced the turquoise water, separated from the sea by a wide strip of white sand beach, and was nearly deserted this early in the day. I studied the lunch menu, written in chalk above the bar, and decided it looked like a good place to return to.

Out on the sand, a family of four was setting up for the day—kids with floaties and flippers, mom wielding a bottle of sunscreen while dad set up an umbrella. All four were pasty white, and I guessed it was their first day of vacation after a winter spent indoors.

My soft drink was half gone when I heard a male voice behind me, and the waitress who'd given me the Coke was telling him I wanted to see him. I turned to see a guy who was probably a little younger than I—maybe thirty at the most. He had blond hair bleached by hours in the sun and a perma-tan from beach living.

I slid off my stool and held out my hand. "Peter?"

He nodded, a crooked little smile brightening his features.

Rather than go into the whole spiel about Jenna's possible reasons for being there, I simply handed over her photo. "Ever seen her? It would have been about thirteen years ago."

For half a second, his eyes widened.

"She's been here." I didn't pose it as a question.

"Oh gosh, yes. I didn't think I'd ever see her again."

My heartbeat picked up—my first solid lead. "Look

carefully. Are you sure it's the same woman?"

His eyes met mine, then went back to the photo. "Definitely." His big grin revealed nice, even teeth in a smile that probably nabbed him lots of dates. "And yes, thirteen years ago."

"You've got a great memory."

"I was seventeen. She looked like a model. What guy wouldn't remember that, especially since she was so genuine. I mean, totally *not* full of herself like a lot of girls."

"Did she remain here, on the island?"

"I wish."

"Maybe I should have asked, how long was she here?"

He shrugged. "Couple of days, maybe. I really don't know."

"Did you talk to her? Do you know anything else about her story?"

"Um … we talked, yeah. But we didn't really *talk.* Know what I mean?"

I nodded, encouraging him to go on.

"Well, I asked where she was from, kind of standard chat when you're in a tourist place like this. She dodged the question, asked me what was the best way to the mainland. Which, now that I think about it was kind of weird. Everyone who comes to this island—most Americans, anyway—arrive in Belize on the mainland and then either get a flight or a boat to bring them to Ambergris."

"Did she say anything else?"

"Not much. Pretty quiet, kept staring around, like she was nervous."

"You said she stayed around for a couple of days. So she came in the bar more than once?"

"Three times. All of them memorable in my teenage

mind." Again, the winsome smile. "Second time, she wanted lunch but hadn't exchanged any money at the airport. Asked if we took American dollars, and I said yes. She ordered the lobster roll. Third time, well, she didn't exactly come into the bar, but I saw her walking along the beach. She seemed sort of lost, like she had no purpose. I don't know … that's not exactly right either."

"Did she ever tell you her name?"

"Sadie. But I called her that when she came back the second time, and she didn't answer. I kind of got the feeling it was made up. She seemed like a really private person."

"Did you get anything else—overhear anything between her and another patron?"

He shook his shaggy blond head. "Like I said, really private. She didn't chat up anyone else at all."

I gave Peter my card and asked him to call if he thought of any other little facts. I held out my hand and he seemed reluctant to give up the photo of Jenna. I teased him a little about this being the one that got away.

I walked out the beachside entrance to the bar and walked along the same path Jenna must have taken. I felt a surge of excitement—my first proof that Jenna had survived her fall into the sea. But what had I really learned? Not a whole lot. Nothing to tell me she hadn't lost her memory or even whether she ever went back to America.

Although she hadn't stayed on Ambergris—Peter would have definitely known if she had—she could have found her way to the Belize mainland and from there could have gone anyplace in the world. I thought of Herbert Jones and wondered if he was having any luck with Jenna sightings in Belize City. It could be that Jenna really had been in the country all this time. Maybe she'd seen the accident as a chance to disappear and start over. It wasn't impossible.

As I passed a row of shops near the harbor, I spotted the gift shop Tomasina had recommended. Even though I didn't picture Jenna making gift shop purchases during her stay here, I stepped inside. Racks and tables held a huge selection of all the things tourists like to take home from vacation, from shot glasses, figurines, shells and rocks, to t-shirts, baggy shorts, and logo-wear. Everything was well organized and immaculate.

A tall black woman with neatly braided hair looked up from her computer. "Can I help you?" she asked.

"Are you Maria?" I explained that Tomasina had sent me, and I was looking for information on a woman who might have passed through here years before. I showed her Jenna's photo. Maria adjusted her glasses and studied it for a long time.

"You know, I do think I remember her," she said finally. "Came in to buy a plane ticket."

"Plane ticket? I think you lost me."

Maria tilted her head back and laughed. "Ah, well. I guess that was a few businesses ago. My shop here was once a travel agency."

I had to laugh with her. "Tomasina told me. Said she couldn't remember what enterprise you had going here thirteen years ago."

"Come with me, back to my office," Maria said, turning toward a curtained doorway.

In stark contrast to the neat shelves of the shop, we stepped into a room that made the word 'messy' seem positively plain. A large worktable in the middle was completely covered with gift wrap and ribbons, craft supplies, file folders. Boxes were stacked around all the perimeter walls—to the ceiling—most labeled sketchily in black marker. A sort of system with chaos as part of it.

"Give me a moment," Maria said, turning to survey the space. After a minute or so, she headed toward the lefthand corner. She pulled a box labeled Travels Galore from a tall pile of them.

"My daughter tells me I never throw anything away. She refuses to step into this room."

The daughter had a point.

She carried the box to the worktable and shoved a few other things aside. "Now, where are my client records? ... Bear with me."

Frankly, I was amazed Maria even knew where to begin. The search took about ten minutes, and then she straightened up and held out a sheet of paper.

"Here you go. That's her itinerary."

Chapter 8

How long would it take him to find her, she wondered, staring out at the heavy forest beyond her windows. Years passed and she'd felt safer. Multiple moves, subtle changes in her appearance.

She poured water from the steaming kettle on the stove, then cupped her tea mug, warming her hands as she stared out the small window above the kitchen sink.

"You've been safe, for years now," she said aloud to the walls as she paced her living space. "Keep your ear to the ground, eyes on the news. Don't take chances."

Her gaze fell to the one memento she'd kept, a picture of a dear three-year-old with blond curls, and her heart bled, again. She took the framed photo and put it in a drawer. Some days it simply evoked too many memories.

The trip to Disneyland. Families laughing together,

kids staring in awe at the real-life versions of their cartoon heroes. She'd relaxed her guard, getting into the joy of it all. Watching her little one giggle at the animated creatures in the Small World tunnel, seeing the pure fun all around her.

And then he'd struck.

As always, once the baby was asleep and unaware, father and mother became pitted against one another. The words were harsh, the threats real, and the wounds were internal. It didn't mean they hurt any less.

She'd been punished for her outlook on life, her joy in her child. For what he suspected she knew.

Now, she rushed to the closet, where a flat box under the floor held printed pages of everything she'd saved to the flash drive. She set her tea aside and opened the box. The evidence was still there. A safe deposit box in another city held the original drive. She'd paid enough cash to keep the bank box for fifteen years, time she'd spent waiting, watching.

She set the box back in its hidden spot under the flooring. A month ago, she'd heard something on the TV, news which gave her hope that the time was right.

Would she be a fool to travel outside her special little world here? What *was* she thinking?

Chapter 9

I walked out of the jetway at the Albuquerque Sunport, glad to be home after my layover dragged out many extra hours. Drake had planned to pick me up but now, arriving late, he'd had to take a job so it was Ron waiting for me outside the security area.

"Nothing from Atlanta," he said by way of greeting.

I'd called him the minute I got the travel agent's itinerary for Jenna Farber. Except that she'd traveled under the name of Nancy Miller. With that information, Ron said he would reach out to a private investigator he knew in Georgia, and along with running his own background checks, would see if either of them could come up with a location for either Jenna or Nancy. I felt further deflated when he said there was nothing at that end, and that there were thousands of Nancy Millers in the country.

"Maybe with a bit more time?" I suggested as we rode the escalator down to the baggage claim.

He shook his head. "We're not giving up, but if Atlanta's where she ended up, she's done an amazing job of staying hidden."

In today's world of credit cards, online banking, and the need to present identification for all sorts of transactions, it was nearly impossible for a person to remain completely under the radar. She wouldn't have been able to get a job, file taxes, travel, rent an apartment, or buy a home. There are a thousand ways *someone* can always find us.

"Tell me again, everything that travel agent in Belize said," Ron asked, keeping an eye toward the bags circling on the metal carousel.

I described the gift shop and the quirky Maria, who'd run a variety of businesses. "It's amazing she pulled the travel itinerary at all, as messy as that storage room was. But she did. As she recalled the day Jenna came in, Maria told me Jenna wanted to leave as soon as possible and that she had no luggage. A small backpack was it. She laughed a little and said most tourists travel with way too much luggage. She told me of one woman who'd come with three huge suitcases and two tote bags, for a week's stay. How much space does your bikini and a cover-up take, anyway?"

Speaking of luggage, my suitcase appeared. Ron retrieved it and we walked out toward the parking garage.

"So, anyway, this stranger with no luggage booked a flight to Atlanta. Her passport was in the name of Nancy Miller, but it did appear to be Jenna in the picture. Maria assumed she lived there or was meeting family, based on the way 'Nancy' talked."

Ron unlocked the Mustang and put my bag in the trunk. "It sounds logical that she would choose a destination where she had contacts, but why not just come on home?"

I fell into the passenger seat as he started the car. "I'm starting to get the feeling Jenna's home life was not entirely happy. Little things both Maria and the bartender said, based on the way she acted and how she talked."

"Such as?"

"Nervous. Looking around, all the time, as if she was worried about being spotted. And she was very cagey about what she revealed in conversation. Basically, she shared nothing personal."

"Weird, because for someone who'd just survived falling overboard from a large ship, anyone would assume she would *want* to be found and reunited with her husband."

"Exactly. I'm really beginning to wonder if Talbot has been using us to find Jenna for some darker reason."

Ron pulled onto Gibson Boulevard and concentrated on merging onto the ramp for I-25. "But now, so much time has passed. She'd been declared legally dead after seven years. It's not as if she could reappear with some kind of 'Hi, honey, I'm home' greeting."

"I suppose stranger things have happened. Maybe she'd lost her memory and didn't know how to get home."

"Yet she knew how to come up with a passport and book a flight to the US. And the watchfulness. I just have this feeling she headed for Atlanta because someone there could help her stay hidden."

"What are you thinking?" I asked. "Witness protection?"

He shook his head. "To get government support and into a witness protection program, she'd have to be a high-profile witness in some kind of criminal case. I've checked all the basics about Talbot, and he's never been arrested—other than for a verbal altercation with a traffic cop once."

"Okay then, what if she staged her own disappearance

and created a new identity?"

"Charlie, that takes lots of planning. Buying a fake passport? You gotta really know somebody, for that level of disguise. It's way beyond what your average fashion model turned socialite could manage."

I had to laugh. The idea of someone like Jenna Farber being *average* was a little strange. Although, she certainly had access to plenty of money.

We arrived at my house ten minutes later. "Want to come in? Drake's in Trinidad tonight, getting organized for a sunrise flight tomorrow."

But it seemed we'd covered all the new information about the Farber case for the moment, and I could feel my exhaustion in every pore.

"Get some rest," Ron said. "I'm going to check further into Talbot's business and property holdings. I suddenly have a feeling there's a lot he's not telling us."

Freckles greeted me from her crate, wiggling every inch of her furry little body. I set my suitcase beside the door and let her out, surrendering to a barrage of doggy kisses, ruffling her fur and talking baby talk for a minute or so. She led me to the kitchen, where we helped ourselves to a few treats.

After sending a text to let Drake know I was safely back at home, I wheeled my suitcase to the bedroom and parked it in a corner. A shower and clean jammies, and I was ready to crash for the night. Freckles jumped up to Drake's empty side of the bed and I promised not to tell, as I turned out the light.

The insistent ringing of the landline phone jarred me awake. It's on Drake's side of the bed, and I scrambled over Freckles to reach it. No good news comes in the middle of the night, especially on this line. With a racing heart, I grabbed for the receiver in the dark.

As soon as I said hello, there was a distinct click at the other end and the line went dead.

What the heck? I looked at the bedside clock and saw it was 1:14 a.m. I'd been asleep less than three hours. Ugh. My mind began racing. Okay, yes, it might have just been a wrong number. Or a misdial, although I like to hope the person at the other end would at least apologize. I tried to tell myself it was likely a drunk trying to call a cab, or give it some other kindly spin, but my trip and the investigation was still too fresh in my mind. My darker inclination was to believe it had something to do with the case.

I lay back against my pillow, eyes closed, trying to think positive thoughts about clouds and fields of lavender and other such relaxing topics. When I next looked at the clock, fifteen minutes had passed and I was so wide awake there was no hope for quietly drifting off again. I groaned, turned on a lamp, and swung my legs over the bedside.

Freckles, thinking it must be time to get up, leaped off the side of the bed and raced toward the kitchen. When I didn't follow, she turned around and tried again.

"It's not time for breakfast," I told her, "not even close."

Nevertheless, when I went to the kitchen and reached for the box of chamomile tea, the dog took up a position beside her bowl.

"Seriously? Can't you tell how dark it is outside?"

It didn't matter. And I gave in by dropping a small handful of kibble into her bowl. While the kettle heated, I went back to the bedroom and emptied my suitcase, dumping the clothes into the laundry basket; toiletries went into the bathroom, and I set up my laptop on the dining table. With the cup of tea at my side, I spent a few minutes catching up on emails before the real reason for my unrest caught up and I switched over to my browser.

Ron had all kinds of inside sources for background checks and that's the direction he would go, while looking for more information about Talbot and Jenna Farber, especially Talbot's business ventures. I could take the other direction—social.

I tried to think as Kiley would, in choosing social media outlets where she was likely to hang out, but I have to confess that it's hard to get into the head of a teen these days. After some frustrating minutes, I defaulted back to the ones I would use, on the theory that Jenna was closer to my age and would likely be on one of the platforms I already knew.

Of course, she wasn't. Not under her own name, anyway. I tried the Nancy Miller persona and came up with—no surprise—hundreds of them. Of those who stated they were in the Atlanta area, the Denver area, or anyplace in New Mexico, none of their profile pictures looked anything like Jenna. I even allowed for changes of hair color and style, but I had to admit that Jenna's natural beauty would never allow her to pass for an ordinary grandmother from the South.

I did manage to stumble across Talbot Farber and, by extension, his mother, on Facebook. Talbot's presence was so obviously managed by a publicist who was getting all the right messages out about his business ventures. Grace Farber, on the other hand, posted little family tidbits, including Kiley's activities. Grace had hundreds of friends, so I sent her a friend request, hoping she'd assume I was someone in her circle.

While waiting for her acceptance of me, I mulled over what I would do with the information if I got anything. My main thought was that perhaps Jenna would have used this same approach, and she might be lurking within Grace's group, catching news about her daughter. It would take me a while to go through all of Grace's friends and look at their profiles, but I might spot Jenna and learn something.

Then again, she could very well have adopted a cartoon avatar as herself and provided a completely made-up bio. At that thought, I felt a huge yawn welling up inside me and knew it was time to give sleep another try.

* * *

A thousand birds seemed to be chirping all at once when I opened my eyes to the first light of dawn. Spring was definitely here. I reached wistfully toward Drake's side of the bed, even knowing it was empty. Freckles was snoring on the soft rug beside the bed, and I carefully stepped over her to get to the bathroom.

Teeth brushed, hair combed, and comfy slippers on my feet, I headed toward the kitchen. The dog was right at my heels, heading toward the cupboard where her food is stored. I insisted she go outside to tend to business first, and I walked out into the sunny spring morning with her.

"Charlie? Are you out here?" came Elsa's voice.

I spotted her in her back yard, already dressed and wearing her favorite gardening hat. I waved across the way.

"Dottie and I have just harvested our first crop of spring lettuce," she said. "Would you like some?"

It didn't really matter. She was already on her way over with a basket of freshly picked greens. If I demurred, she would keep offering until I accepted them. Besides, a salad would make an excellent dinner tonight, after my recent binge of travel food. I asked about her health and gave her a quick rundown about my trip to Belize, not bothering with details that didn't matter to her.

By now, Freckles was pestering to go inside for the breakfast she knew was coming. I told Elsa I'd be at the office today, in case she needed anything.

"Drake should be home in a day or so," I told her. "We'll look for a nice weather day ahead and have you and Dottie over for a cookout or something."

She brightened, reminding me that the simplest things can add a lot to an older person's day. I went in and stored the greens in the fridge, fed the dog, and savored my first cup of coffee while putting on jeans and a lightweight sweater. A touch of lipstick, a quick trick to pull my hair up into a messy bun, and I was pretty much ready to leave.

Again, Ron was already at the Victorian when I arrived. He seemed to be taking the Farber case more seriously now. I pulled a muffin from the bakery box I'd picked up on the way, poured another coffee, and shifted the armful as I carried my laptop upstairs to my office.

"Hey, what's up?" he asked as I passed his doorway. "Didn't expect to see you this early."

"Yeah, well. I guess my brain is still in another time zone. What brings you in at this hour?"

He looked up from his computer screen. "The deeper I dig, the interesting-er it gets."

"What do you mean? Talbot Farber?"

"Yeah. It appears the guy is into a whole lotta stuff that goes way beyond selling cars."

"You've got my attention," I said, setting my laptop case on the floor outside his door and carrying my breakfast in with me. I parked myself in the chair in front of his desk.

"A search of the State Corporation Commission records shows Farber as president of two corporations, in addition to the one that operates the dealerships."

I shrugged. "Lots of people own more than one business."

"So I looked up each one, with the addresses on file. One of those addresses is a mail drop—I know this from previous cases—one of those places where no actual business is conducted. It's just a place to collect mail."

I thought of the way our own volume of paper mail had dropped in recent years. Everything is done online, by email or text. Even meetings take place online any more. "Maybe he set that one up ages ago?"

"Maybe. But corporations have to file a report every two years, stating and reaffirming details like this. Unless he has let it slip through the cracks, he's probably still using that address."

"And so …? I don't know what that means."

"Maybe nothing. Yet. The second mysterious corporation definitely seems like a shell. They both could be. I did a few different searches, and neither of them show up with an online presence. What business these days doesn't have a website? There's not a trace of them."

"Again, what does that mean?"

"Creating a business that doesn't appear to actually conduct business … it's often a sign of something illegal going on."

"And what type of illegal things do you think Talbot is into?"

"At this point, no idea. But from our viewpoint, the main question would be whether Jenna Farber knew about them."

"Were those corporations formed while she was still in the picture?"

"Yes. Both of them."

Chapter 10

She pulled on her warm parka and boots, praying her car would start as she stepped past a deep muddy puddle. Spring was definitely not her favorite time of year.

It hadn't always been that way. There was the trip to New York. The flowering trees in Central Park had been abundant, and her normal aversion to crowds and traffic were set aside as she reveled in the positive mood that seemed to fill the city as the weather warmed after a long winter.

They'd booked a suite at the Carlyle and shopped at Tiffany and Bloomingdale's. It was where she'd tried on what became her favorite gown, heavy with beads of deep blue and silver.

"It'll be perfect for the Santa Fe Opera fundraiser next week, honey!" she'd exclaimed.

"Get it. Get the other one too." He pulled out the Amex Black and turned to the awestruck young clerk. "Box them up and have them delivered to the Carlyle."

They had dinner that evening at Le Cirque and, later, orchestra seats at the Winter Garden for *Phantom of the Opera*. The air was balmy as they waited in the queue for their limo afterward. He'd become irritated at the wait. She'd ignored his mood and simply savored the delights of their three days in the city.

Back at the hotel, he'd taken a phone call. Hoping for a romantic evening and the right moment to deliver her news, she'd changed into her filmiest negligee and waited in the bedroom. Their life was a fairytale—all her friends said so. Soon, there would be a baby. His parents would be delighted when they found out. The timing had been his idea, and her hope was that this new little life would smooth out the rough edges she'd begun to feel in the marriage. A couple years into any relationship, inevitable cracks began to appear, didn't they? They were still settling into their life together, and this would make everything perfect.

She'd settled back onto the luxuriously appointed bed, but when he returned from the suite's living room his face was a storm cloud.

Her foot landed in a puddle as she reached for the door handle on her ten-year-old Ford. The New York memory zapped into the past, like a fragile soap bubble that popped at the faintest touch.

She sighed.

No, her life was not at all like it had once been. Thank God. Despite the lack of creature comforts now, she felt her work was important, and she—mostly—felt safe. There was only one thing she desperately wanted now.

Chapter 11

I mulled over what Ron had said about the two corporations, trying to piece together the implications. Logically, it seemed Talbot must have other business interests that he wanted, or needed, to keep separated from his auto dealerships.

Could be something as simple as a completely different line of commerce. Could be anything from an animal shelter to an art gallery, or a charitable foundation to help needy kids. Any of those—anything at all, really—would legitimately operate completely separate from his main business. But why, then, hadn't he listed the purpose for each of those entities in more specific terms?

Part of setting up a business was a requirement to state the nature of the business. Farber Auto Sales, Inc, as the parent company of all the dealerships, clearly stated that sales and related services pertaining to automobiles was their business purpose. These other two—they listed only the most general of terminology: To conduct and maintain business with a variety of clientele.

What on earth did that even mean? Maybe I should just call Talbot and come right out and ask him.

I was at my desk, my muffin half finished, trying to parse the words while a brown and white spaniel face stared at me in hopes that the unfinished part of my meal would suddenly drop into her reach.

Ron appeared in my doorway. "Another interesting tidbit. Had to go county-by-county to find this, but Farber also owns a thousand-acre ranch just south of Santa Fe."

"As in, a working ranch? Has he suddenly become a cattleman?"

"Doubtful. But it could be interesting to check it out. Maybe from the air?"

"Got it. I'll suggest it to Drake the next time I talk to him. We'll need coordinates, landmarks, some way to spot it."

"I'm sure I can find a map of some kind." He walked back to his own office, leaving me to hand muffin bits to the dog.

Another thought occurred to me, and I walked across the hall to interrupt Ron once again. "Don't we owe Talbot a report on what we're doing up to this point?"

His expression told me he was thinking along the same lines. We were investigating our own client's background, when he expected we were looking into his wife's movements.

"He'll know part of it as soon as we present him with your travel expenses to Belize. Let me draft a report about that aspect of it, and we'll see what he says." He picked up a pen and jotted himself a note. "For now, let's keep quiet about what we've discovered about these corporations and the ranch. We'd better see where those lead. I'll chalk up the billing to 'investigative online time' or some such. You're the accountant. Figure out what expense category works best."

I could do that.

I sent a quick text to Drake: Let me know when you're heading this way. Got a question.

Then I went back to my office to gather my travel receipts and make a list of them. An hour disappeared, as they tend to do, but I did have a completed billing for Talbot Farber, showing the retainer he'd paid and how much of it we had used.

My phone rang as I was looking up the address for the billing.

"Hey, hon," said Drake. "I'm on my way home. What's up?"

I briefly explained Ron's idea that we check out the Farber ranch from the air. "I don't have the exact location yet, though."

"That's okay. I need to plan that trip for another day. We've got weather moving into the higher elevations, and it could be snowy around Santa Fe by this afternoon."

"Good point. I'll see you at home later."

I should have thought of the weather aspect of it. April is an iffy month, especially in the northern mountains. A lot of those places spend a month dealing with snow, then mud, then wind, then snow again. By the time Ron got the coordinates for the ranch, Drake would have a chance to look ahead and choose a good day for the flight.

"Charlie—can you come here a second?" came Ron's voice.

I stood and stretched the kinks out of my back and shoulders.

"Want to get out of the office for a while?"

Is the Pope Catholic? Of course I would love to get out in the fresh air.

"It's a stakeout."

My happy balloon deflated. Stakeouts are the worst.

"That mail drop location. Staking it out can't last forever. They're only open nine-to-five."

And it was already nearly noon. "I need to watch for Talbot picking up his mail?"

"Could be that, but more than likely he doesn't pick it up himself. There's probably a secretary or some kind of errand runner."

"And then what? Follow them?"

He gave that some thought. "We already know who rents the box. What we need to know is what he's receiving there."

"So I should follow this pickup person until they accidentally drop a piece of mail? Ron ..."

"You're resourceful, sis. Figure out something."

"Give me his box number," I said with a sigh.

Exactly nine minutes later, I was pulling up outside Mail Services Unlimited on Lomas Boulevard. I walked over to the wall of mailboxes with all the confidence of a customer and quickly scanned to find the number of the one I wanted. Through the tiny glass window, I could see there were envelopes inside. Good. No one had picked it up yet today.

And, as luck would have it, there was a clear view of the parking lot through the front window. I went back out to my Jeep and settled in.

I'd deliberately parked on the second row, nearer to the street, to be less noticeable to any diligent employee inside the mail place. For more than an hour, people came and went. I saw them go inside, check their boxes, and leave right away. A few went up to the customer service window at the far end of the space and came out with packages.

No sign of Talbot Farber. No one else approached the box where I had my binoculars aimed. I was about to reach for the bag of chips I'd brought along for fortification when I noticed someone different from the others. A kid of about nineteen got out of a van with Pickup and Delivery Service neatly lettered on the side.

Something told me to follow him, so I did.

Inside, he pulled out a ring with more than a dozen keys on it. His routine started him at the lefthand end of the wall of mailboxes. He opened a box, pulled out the mail, flipped through to see if there was a notice of a package, and stuck the envelopes into a messenger bag that appeared to have divided sections inside.

I hovered down the way, a few feet from the box I knew to be Talbot's, a brilliant plan (if I do say so myself) beginning to form in my mind.

The moment the courier pulled up the key for Talbot's box and inserted it, I dashed over to him, breathless and agitated.

"Ohmygosh, I'm so glad you're here. I need my envelope back."

"What?" He had an inch-thick clump of envelopes in his hand, most appearing to come from individuals since they were a hodgepodge of sizes and colors.

"I didn't mean to mail it yet, and I'm going to be in so much trouble."

He didn't even have the good sense to turn away or hide the envelopes from my view. "Who are you, anyway?"

I spotted the return address on the topmost piece. "Renata Sanchez. Oh! That's it, right there! That's me!"

I didn't even give the guy a chance to react. I simply grabbed the envelope. The others scattered to the floor, and by the time he'd clocked what was going on, I ran from the building. He couldn't very well follow. There was mail all over the floor.

While he stooped to pick everything up, I dashed out and disappeared around the side of the building. *Clever, Charlie, not walking directly out to my own vehicle.* I watched from my hiding place until the courier finished his duties and drove away in his van.

Inside my Jeep, Freckles was having a fit. She'd seen me run, and now she wanted in on the fun part.

"Don't worry, baby," I told her. "We'll do something good now."

With nothing more than a muffin and about six potato chips for the day, I'd decided we would stop off for fast food on our way back to the office. I pulled through the McDonald's drive-thru, getting my usual Big Mac and a small burger, plain, for my assistant.

Back at the office, Ron kind of gave me the side-eye when I told him how I'd ingeniously nabbed a clue to the puzzle of the mailboxes. His expression went a little more toward impressed when he actually opened the envelope.

"A money order," he said. "The notation on it just says Pmt #25."

"Okay …"

He examined the envelope, the addresses on it, and the money order. "It's made out to one of the corporations we found linked to Talbot. And payment number twenty-five. Someone's been paying a long time for something."

I was still puzzled. "Like what?"

He gave a shrug. "No idea what they're paying for, but this smacks of loan sharking. And I'd guess the payer is falling behind. It's an even dollar amount. Two hundred dollars."

"Because a payment with interest is normally some oddball amount. And once they can't make the exact payment anymore, they resort to paying whatever they can."

"You got it."

"It could explain how Talbot privately supplements his dealership income. Maybe his shell corporation is acting as a finance company?"

"With exorbitant interest rates for people whose credit scores are so bad they'd never qualify for financing through the normal channels."

"Is that illegal?"

"It is if the interest rates are way outside the norm. Or if he's using scare tactics and intimidation to collect."

"Ron, we can't let this poor lady get in any worse trouble. Seal the envelope back up and I'll return it. I can just tell the mail clerk I found it on the floor."

"Make a copy first, just in case we end up needing to present evidence to law enforcement. And then I've got more news."

* * *

Ron's other news consisted of a list of the politically powerful and important people in the state who were in tight with Talbot Farber. Some of this came as no surprise, but I still took Ron's warning seriously.

"You and Drake be careful when you fly over that ranch. Don't let yourself get caught making low passes over the place or taking pictures."

"But we want pictures, right?" Then it clicked with me. "You're thinking about that Epstein guy who was running a sex trafficking operation down south, with lots of the rich and powerful as clients."

He waggled a hand back and forth. "Could be something like that."

"If that were the case, I can't understand why Talbot hired us. Did he actually think Jenna's whereabouts are the only thing we'd look at?"

"Probably. You've dealt with rich people before. They start thinking they're immune to any kind of punishment. And they always think they're smarter than everyone else. It's the very thing that gets them caught."

Valid point.

Ron straightened in his chair and switched off his computer. "More than likely, you'll find a solar or wind farm, some legit moneymaker for Talbot. I'm just saying, stay alert."

* * *

The storm passed through the state during the night. Drake was safely back home well before it hit, and in the morning, he checked the weather maps. We'd settled on the living room sofa with our coffee.

"Looks like the snow fell above eight-thousand feet, so we should be able to cover anything in the Santa Fe area. You got the coordinates for this place?"

I handed him the notes Ron had given me. "You're

sure you want to do this?"

"Absolutely. Half the fun of being married to you is all the adventures you get me into."

"And the other half …?"

His eyes cut toward the bedroom door. "Hey! I meant our life here together, not merely in one room."

I gave him a light jab in the ribs, followed by a kiss. "Me too. You and our life together are the most important thing."

He returned his attention to the coordinates for the ranch. "You believe Talbot Farber is up to something, and I can't sit by while corruption goes unpunished. And I know how much this case means to you." He squeezed my hand back.

I blinked back grateful tears. "Thank you. Yeah, there's something about that teenage girl that really touched me."

Drake broke in gently. "I'll take every precaution. Don't worry, Charlie. Let's focus on finding out if there's some connection at that ranch to the missing woman you're looking for."

I managed a shaky smile. "Okay, let's do this."

Drake grinned. "Now tell me what you need me to do."

I outlined a tentative plan as we finished our coffee, buoyed by Drake's steadiness as my life partner. He really is the best.

I took a deep breath and jumped into the details. "So, for the flight, I need aerial photos of the whole property—any buildings, vehicles, activity. Especially near the canyon on the south end. I'll fly with you and concentrate on taking the pictures."

Drake nodded. "I can do low passes with the helicopter cameras. Should get decent pictures, as long as no one starts taking potshots."

"We have to be careful. Don't take any risks."

"I won't," Drake assured me. "I know that area pretty well. There are some box canyons we can follow, stay out of sight."

I relaxed a little, trusting his experience.

"Got it. We'll look for any unusual activity, see if we can figure out what it's about." Drake refilled our mugs from the French press on the coffee table. "What else do you need?"

I stirred sugar into my coffee, considering. "Ron's trying to find info on Talbot's finances and holdings." I told him briefly about the two mysterious corporations we'd discovered and the possible loan sharking operation. "It would be terrific if we could come up with hard evidence, something out there at the ranch. If you can get us close enough, maybe you could drop me off if we spot a building that might contain records and computers?"

Drake raised an eyebrow. "That would be trickier. Helicopters aren't exactly silent, and I'm not letting you take any chances." He relaxed a little. "I'll see what I can manage. As we scout the ranch, we'll see if they have any unusual setups. Hangars, buildings not visible from the road."

"Yes! Anything suspicious like that." I felt myself getting excited, my hands gesturing. "And if I can get shots of them meeting with officials, exchanging money ..."

"Bribery caught on camera would make a nice smoking gun for the DA," he said with a grin.

"I think we're getting ahead of ourselves. We have no idea what we'll see out there." I leaned back against the couch cushions.

Drake's expression turned serious. "Do you really think we're up against some dangerous people?"

I chewed at my lip, considering the risks. "I don't know. I think Talbot has connections, lots of them across the state—judges, cops, even politicians in his pocket. Truthfully, I have no idea how far he'd go to stop us."

Drake took my hand, his brow furrowed. "He doesn't know me. Maybe I should handle the surveillance alone ..."

"No." I squeezed his hand. "We do this together."

I know he's just trying to protect me, but there's no way I'm sitting this out. We both have skills to contribute. And I refuse to let Farber intimidate me into backing down.

"If we stick to the plan, watch each other's backs, we can pull this off," I said firmly.

Drake studied me for a moment, then nodded. "All right. But no unnecessary risks. We gather evidence quietly."

By mid-morning we were on our way to the small westside airport, Double Eagle, where Drake's helicopter is hangared. He went through his preflight routine while I rechecked the long-lens camera we'd brought along. Fifteen minutes later, we were buckled into our seats, headsets on, radio check complete.

As Drake started up the aircraft, I glanced at my phone background—a photo of us on our wedding day, smiling and hopeful. No matter what happened, I knew Drake had my back. And I have his.

The rotors whipped up a little dust as we lifted off, and Albuquerque receded below us.

Chapter 12

When was the last time she remembered an April day warm enough to wear summer clothing? The cruise. She could go months at a time without thinking about the cruise itself, but rarely a day without thinking of what she'd lost. Her daughter. Her innocence.

Her wedding day memories came flooding back. Was that truly the last time she felt young and free and innocent?

There was the church, the one her fiancé's parents attended. His brother Graham as best man, her best friend Barb as her maid of honor. They could have gone elaborate, with a ten-foot cake and a dozen attendants each—they certainly had the money and enough friends to fill a large reception hall—but they'd kept it simple. Without her own parents, without California or New York, she was stepping into a whole new world. And on that day, she welcomed it.

Her own parents had died within six months of each other, shortly after she met the man who would change her life. She'd felt as though she was leaving nothing of importance behind. They did fun things as a couple—spur-of-the-moment weekend trips to ski or find a beach or luxury spa somewhere. He introduced her to his hobbies. There was time at the shooting range where they would plink away at targets; he'd purchased her a dirt bike to match his, and they would roar across the open mesa; they cooked massive barbeque dinners together and invited his most important clients. Ahead was a world of lavish homes, fast cars, faster friends and acquaintances. Travel to anyplace she desired. It seemed like a perfect existence.

Two years later, their first child entered the picture. Three years after that, she'd reached such a point of desperation she felt suicidal much of the time. What had gone so wrong with the fairytale?

Chapter 13

Drake made a quick pass over the Talbot ranch, five hundred feet above the ground. We were close enough to grab shots of an elaborate entryway—a stone and wood portal with metal gates, which were standing open at the moment. A winding graveled lane led to a Spanish Colonial ranch house, not dissimilar in style to the city house in the north valley of Albuquerque. We got shots of the circular drive, the portico, and the dwelling. He purposely remained at enough distance to avoid the attention of anyone inside.

To the north of the house stood a garage with four bays, all doors closed, although a large, dark SUV stood outside one of them. To the south, a narrow road led about a quarter of a mile to a large metal building, probably two thousand square feet, maybe more. A wide roll-up door stood open, and a delivery truck was backed up to it. There were no signs or logos on the truck and no humans in evidence, although I felt certain they must be nearby.

I operated the cameras and got it all.

"We don't dare go back, directly over the place, right away," he said, aiming for one of the box canyon areas he'd told me about. "They'll know we're watching them."

"I wonder what the delivery truck brought."

"Can you enlarge the photos enough to see any lettering?" He set the aircraft down gently on a high, level spot at least two miles from the house.

I looked at the camera's monitor and scrolled back through the shots. "It looks completely plain. No way to see the license plate with the back of the truck practically up against the garage opening."

Drake was fiddling with the screen on his GPS, zooming the image out to cover the entire ranch. "According to our aviation map there's a pond and a windmill. Both are closer to the foothills where the terrain starts to rise. Shall we check those out?"

"Wouldn't hurt to see."

We lifted off again, getting an overview of the high desert landscape, mostly sage and scrubby piñon trees. Dual tire tracks led off to the north, and we kept them in sight as we gained about a thousand feet in altitude. From there we could see the pond and windmill. A dozen black cows milled about, not noticing the aircraft. No vehicles or people were anywhere nearby.

"Doesn't look like much of a cattle operation, does it?" I commented.

"Not at all. He's either one of those 'big hat, no cattle' kind of ranchers, or maybe he has leased grazing rights to somebody with a few head to feed for the season."

"He's a car salesman. I have a hard time picturing him as any kind of real rancher."

He gave the helicopter a little bit of right-pedal and we aimed southward. "That bluff ahead is the boundary of his land. Unless you think otherwise, I'm guessing the house and that metal building are about the extent of the operation."

"Agreed. Make one more pass over the house and I'll see if I can spot anything else worth getting pictures. But stay high enough that we don't appear interested."

He laughed at my phrasing, but he knew what to do. We cruised by, as though we were on our way to some important destination. I got more footage of the back and northern face of the house. The tall door on the metal building was closed now, and a man was climbing into the cab of the truck. He looked up briefly, trying to locate the helicopter sound, but we were gone before he had much time to think about it.

"Shall we make a little detour over our cabin before we head in?" Drake asked.

"Sure." I packed the camera back into its case.

Below, he'd located Highway 14 and we tracked it toward the little town of Cerillos, then Madrid and Golden. In the foothills, completely off the grid, sat the little cabin we'd found and purchased a couple years ago. Drake brought the aircraft down eighty yards from the front door.

"Want to go inside?" he asked.

"Better save that for another trip. If I go in, I'll just feel like I have to clean it up and then I'll want to stay the night." The problem with having a mountain cabin that we don't visit often is that it's always dusty and abandoned-feeling when we first get there. "We'd better get back to

Albuquerque and let Ron take a look at the pictures we just shot."

* * *

Sally had left for the day and Ron was warming a burrito in the kitchen microwave when I got back to the office. I held up the chip from the camera.

"Shall we see how much we can enlarge these?"

He peeled the wrapper away from part of the burrito and took a big bite of it as he led the way upstairs.

"Put the chip into the card slot on my computer," he said. "I don't want to get it greasy."

Apparently, he didn't have that same worry about his computer mouse, as he began navigating into the photo program. I kind of rolled my eyes. Note to self: don't touch that mouse.

During the flight I'd put the camera in video mode as we approached the property, then snapped away individual shots of the vehicles and buildings. Those would have the highest resolution, so that's where Ron put his attention now, zooming in tight on the pictures to get the most detail possible.

As Drake and I had discussed, his primary interest was in finding identifying information on the vehicles.

"The SUV has a dealer plate," he said, pointing to the little DL designation on it. "No surprise there."

A minute later he had the side of the delivery truck enlarged. Low on the driver's door was a series of numbers.

"That's the DOT registration number for a commercial vehicle. I'm pretty sure I have a database I can access to find out who operates it."

I gave him a little punch on the shoulder. "And *that's* what we wanted."

"Don't set off the celebratory fireworks just yet," he cautioned. "It may not tell us anything useful."

Thanks for bursting my bubble, I thought as I went into my own office and surveyed my desk to see what awaited me. I'd fallen behind on my accounting duties since the trip to Belize, so I got a few entries caught up and logged into the Taxation & Revenue website to file our monthly report.

Less than thirty minutes passed before Ron was standing in my doorway.

"This might almost be worth some fireworks," he said, holding up a page he'd printed.

"Oh?"

"That DOT identification number. It's registered to a company that's on a federal watch list for weapons violations."

Okay, I must admit I did not see that coming.

Chapter 14

We suspected Farber of making shady loans, maybe even cooking the books a little at the dealerships, but weapons?

Ron plopped onto the sofa by the window in my office. "Let's go over what we think we know about this case."

I nodded, rubbing my temples. "Jenna Farber disappeared from a cruise ship and her husband reported her missing. He claimed she disappeared from their cabin in the middle of the night."

"Right, but we know that's a lie. The news reported the names of those who went overboard during the melee after the fire, and she was the only one not accounted for," Ron said. "You discovered she flew from Belize to Atlanta as Nancy Miller. New identity, probably a new look. Red flag number one."

"Exactly. She was covering her tracks, wanting to stay

hidden for some reason. Then there's Talbot's lie about seeing her recently." I shook my head, anger simmering in my gut. "I think he completely fabricated that story. I don't buy his devotion to Jenna for a minute."

Ron grimaced. "I really don't like losing faith in a client, but even I have to admit he's hiding something. But what?"

"Maybe he believes that private investigators have something like attorney-client privilege, that anything we learn about him can't be revealed."

"And maybe he thinks we have to only uncover those parts of the truth that he wants discovered. Thinks we have to side with him because he's paying us. Talbot probably didn't realize that's not necessarily the case."

"Or his own people discovered the same things and asked if he really wanted all this brought to light."

"We can guess at it all day," Ron said, rising stiffly from the sofa. "But I'll tell you this—I'm not going to ignore his lies and walk away until we know the truth of what really happened to Jenna Farber. Almost anything could have happened to her over the years, and as far as I'm concerned, she's still missing."

"We need more pieces." I stood, ready for action. Time to have a cup of tea and get back to it. "I'm going back to that FAA database we can access. We haven't found any evidence Jenna, or Nancy, stayed in Atlanta. So where did she go next?"

Downstairs in the kitchen, I heated the kettle and found a packet of good quality Assam tea. I filled my mug to the brim, the rich aroma cutting through my fatigue. Back at my desk, I pulled up the flight records again. Starting where I'd left off after she arrived in Atlanta, I scanned forward.

"Okay, Jenna … or Nancy … where did you go from here?" I mused aloud.

My eyes checked the list of outbound flights. Most were domestic routes, but one caught my attention—a flight to London a week after her arrival from Belize.

"Hmm," I murmured. That international hop was odd. What was in London? Then I remembered the background check Ron had done on the Farber family. Talbot's brother, Graham, had taken a job in London after college. Could he still be there?

And, if so, why would Jenna have gone there, rather than simply calling him? Every flight, every airport, presented the danger of her being caught—if she truly wanted to be in hiding.

"Ron, check this out." I carried my laptop into his office. "Jenna—as Nancy Miller—flew to London. That's where Talbot's brother lives. There's our next lead."

Ron's eyebrows shot up. "Well, well. Looks like we need to have a chat with Mr. Graham Farber."

My adrenaline surged. What was Jenna up to with Graham? Did he know something about her disappearance? Could I possibly sneak in a trip to England at Talbot's expense?

Ron leaned back in his chair, rubbing his chin thoughtfully. "So Jenna was traveling under an alias and now it looks like she secretly met up with her husband's brother in London. This definitely suggests she was trying to hide something."

I nodded. "The question is, was she hiding from Talbot, or working with Graham behind Talbot's back?"

"Good point," Ron said. "If she was afraid of Talbot, Graham could have been helping her get away safely. But if they were scheming together ..."

"It could mean Jenna's not as innocent as we think," I finished.

I thought back to our first interview with Talbot. He had seemed so distraught and then hopeful, pleading with us to find his beloved wife. But now I had to wonder—how much of that was an act?

"We've found no evidence that backs up what Talbot said, about seeing Jenna recently," I said. "If he lied about that, why?"

Ron leaned forward, his expression grim. "I think it's time we consider the possibility that Talbot was directly involved in Jenna's disappearance. Maybe even Graham too. We need to research further into both brothers' lives, see what else they might be hiding."

"Did the authorities look at Talbot as a suspect at the time Jenna went overboard?"

"For about five minutes. Maybe. Others from the ship testified how chaotic it was, how people were afraid of the fire, jumping into the water. The cruise line just wanted the whole mess to go away, and it looked like the official ruling was that one passenger unfortunately succumbed in the sea."

I felt a chill run down my spine. Were we dealing with a cunning killer who had fooled us all? Was Jenna hiding from a dangerous man? Or was Jenna pulling a fast one on everybody? No matter which, we had to tread carefully.

"Let's keep this between us for now," I told Ron. "We don't know who we can trust. We've got a lot of evidence, but we still don't know how any of it ties together."

He nodded. "I have a feeling we'll get this, Charlie. If Jenna's alive, we'll find her and figure out what's going on."

"I think we need to talk to Graham Farber."

"If I can track him down," Ron said, turning back to his computer.

Chapter 15

It took Ron more than a day to get Graham Farber's London phone number and set up a video call with him. We both wanted to be in on this one. At the appointed time, I set up a chair next to Ron's and we appeared on his computer screen. Within a few seconds the connection was made and Graham greeted us.

First impression: Graham was a younger, softer version of Talbot. Same jawline, same smile, less gray in his hair. Either he'd always been more casual, or the years of living in Britain had changed him. He wore a deep blue Henley shirt and his hair was slightly longer, almost to his collar, and fashionably mussed. And, although American, his voice had picked up a slight British accent.

From something Talbot had said in one of our encounters, he and Graham weren't close. Still, I had cautioned Ron that we didn't know that whatever we said here could get directly back to our client. We began the conversation with the basics, introducing ourselves as investigators who'd been hired to find out if Jenna survived her ordeal at sea.

Graham's face remained passive as we talked.

"We've discovered that Jenna did, in fact, survive," Ron carefully told him, watching his expression the whole time. "Now we're looking into where she might have gone after leaving Belize, via Atlanta, and it seems she traveled to London at one point."

Graham nodded in a noncommittal way.

I took the compassionate tone. "Graham, if she came there to see you, and if you can shed any light on what happened next, we'd love to know. I've been in touch with her daughter, and Kiley is hurting. She wants to know what happened to her mom. Talbot has ... um, maybe not been as supportive as he could, in that area."

At the mention of Kiley, he softened. And when I mentioned Talbot's attitude, Graham's mouth opened as if he wanted to say something.

We waited in silence, letting him put his thoughts together.

After about a minute, Ron spoke again. "If you're worried that whatever you say may be repeated to Talbot, don't. Our investigation has already put us in doubt on several statements he's made. At this point, we're most concerned about Jenna and her daughter."

Something in Graham's expression relaxed. He sat back in his chair, thinking, then leaned forward again. "All right, yes. Jenna did come here. This was about two weeks after the event on the ship."

"You saw her?"

"Yes, of course. Not to say I wasn't completely stunned when she called me from Heathrow and said she wanted to meet."

"So Talbot had informed you his wife was missing?"

"My parents did. My brother and I don't really talk."

"My big question, now, is did Jenna stay? Is she still in England?" I asked.

"Oh, no. Well, not so far as I know. She'd come in with a passport in another name, would have had to go through some fairly complex requirements to get an extended visa to live and work here. But aside from that, I gathered she planned to return to the States."

"What did she want from you?" I backtracked. "Sorry, that sounded harsh. Can you take us through the conversations, what she told you, what kind of help she was looking for?"

He leaned back in his chair slightly, shifting his gaze upward as he recalled the events.

"I invited her to my flat but she said no, someone could be watching. She would take a cab and meet me at a pub. She didn't even say what hotel she would be staying at. I don't know if, at that point, she'd actually made a plan for accommodations. So, we met a few hours later at a place near Trafalgar Square."

"How did she seem?"

"She was extremely jittery. I'm no psychologist, but I got the feeling she was only a hair's breadth from a mental breakdown. I bought her a meal, let her do the talking."

"And what did she tell you?"

"The marriage was a sham. She knew things she wasn't supposed to know about her husband and his business dealings, and that Talbot had tried to kill her."

"So he threw her off the cruise ship?"

"She didn't say that, specifically. Understand, she was rambling, exhausted, and mentally not at her best. I gathered that a large insurance policy on her life was part of what made her believe my brother would rather see her dead."

"Did she say what kinds of things she 'knew' that would cause trouble?"

"Again, not specifically." His expression became troubled. "I just felt so badly for her. I—"

Ron and I sat quietly, giving him a moment.

Graham leaned forward, rubbing his face with both hands. "You see, I had a bit of a secret crush on Jenna, even before her wedding. It was all I could do to attend as Talbot's best man and watch her marry him. But my brother is a force of nature, as they say, and there was no way I could declare my feelings to her. She was smitten with him, and I would never reveal what I'd witnessed as a boy, about the way he treats those in his inner circle. I simply had to stand back and watch as she bound herself to him with vows. It was for my own peace of mind that I accepted the position here in the UK and separated myself from the family situation."

Okay, wow. It took me a few seconds to formulate another question.

"Would you have taken her in, kept her there with you?"

He let out a deep breath. "In a heartbeat, even though I knew it would probably end in disaster for both of us, the moment Talbot found out."

"I'm sensing a *but* ..."

"Yeah." He blew out a pent-up breath. "Two things. Jenna had never known about my feelings for her, and I knew that moment, in that pub, was not the time to bare my soul. Secondly, she was nowhere near ready to settle in one place. Her overriding concern at that moment was to somehow get Kiley back, and then to get the two of them to safety. But she had no plan, no resources. She just kept saying that Talbot held all the power, that he'd threatened her if she ever left him or tried to take *his* daughter away."

"So she didn't tell you what she wanted to do next?"

"I didn't push. I assumed she would stay in London for at least a week or two, we'd meet again and discuss options for her."

"And, did she?"

"We met one other time, the following day, at a different pub in the same neighborhood. She said she'd spotted a man outside her hotel and was convinced he was watching her. She needed to get going."

"Where? Did she say?"

"I asked her not to tell me. I'm not proud of it, but my brother and his lot scare me. I was afraid if I knew where Jenna went, they would get the information out of me."

Half of me wanted to applaud his clearheaded thinking; the other half wanted to call him a weenie. "Was there anyone you confided in? Anyone else who knew about Jenna's visit to you?"

Graham shook his head. "I kept that promise, even through visits back to my parents, times when I saw Kiley and her dad together. I couldn't trust any of the adults, and was even worried that Kiley might, in her innocence, say something if she knew for a fact that her mother was alive."

"Was there any other contact between you and Jenna?"

"She texted me that night, after our second meeting. One word: Leaving. And I've heard nothing since. I tried calling the number she'd used, but it obviously was a temporary phone. Calls never went through." He let out a shaky breath. "I've played this in my head, every which way. She was in the process of a mental breakdown and went somewhere for help ... or not. She made it to safety, or she didn't. Talbot caught up with her, or he didn't. Obviously, since he's hired you both, at least we know he hasn't found her on his own."

"True. That's a comfort. I wish we knew more," I said.

We ended the call with the usual plea to let us know if anything else came to mind or if—wishful thinking—he should hear from her again.

Chapter 16

A bitter wind howled through cracks in the cabin walls. She walked to the kitchen and stashed a lovely cut of salmon and some fresh veggies in the fridge. Her face felt chapped, even after the brief foray into town. She went into the bathroom and reached for the jar of her favorite skin cream.

Oh, for the days when the top brands were within her reach—available and financially feasible. She looked into the mirror and spoke aloud to herself.

"And you still would not go back, would you?" A wink as she opened the jar. "No."

Only for one thing. And, as she'd discovered, it was still too risky.

She smoothed the cream over her cheeks and forehead and a sudden memory came to her, an ad poster of herself mounted on the wall at Heathrow airport. She'd almost shrieked and run. Who knew the company was still using her photos in their ad campaigns?

Leaving London had been one of the harder things she'd done. She wanted so much to trust Graham, but he *was* Talbot's brother. And the Farbers stuck together. She'd been a fool to go there, an even bigger fool to see him twice. Especially after she spotted the man in the dark overcoat who was watching her hotel lobby and later appeared in Trafalgar Square, not fifty feet behind her.

She'd taken a taxi out to Heathrow at four a.m. without a real plan in mind. Just get away. Graham's interest had been a little too keen, his offer of help a little *too* willing.

At that stage in her life, anything could be a trap.

Her flight took her to New York, where she realized she would quickly run out of money unless she found immediate work. The other danger there was that her face was too well known; she had too many friends in the city. And so, she ran again. A bus to Detroit. A train from Toronto to Vancouver.

She stopped using the new Nancy Miller credit card, spent cash from her dwindling supply, presented her ID only when it was absolutely required, got away with things because she could flash a winning smile at a porter or driver. She wore no makeup and changed direction whenever she spotted one of the images of her formerly glamorous self.

Her hair was shorter by then, and a different color. She dressed in the plainest of clothing and kept her eyes downcast most of the time. Rarely, someone gave her a second glance. Few presumed to ask if she was Jenna Caldwell, the model. If they did, the answer was simple and delivered with an incredulous chuckle, "No, sorry."

She'd come to love her new, simpler look and lifestyle. Each of the wonderful memories from her married years came with its own horror story attached, and she'd had no problem giving them up.

Only one thing still tugged at her heart. Her desire to fix it was very real, but she'd still not come up with a viable plan. Other than time.

Chapter 17

When the video screen went dark, Ron and I looked at each other. Now what? It was the question in both of our minds. Obviously, Graham would have an interest in keeping Jenna safe, but we both had the feeling he'd been truthful about not knowing her whereabouts.

"Well, I guess it's back to the FAA records," I said, relishing the idea as much as I would a root canal.

"At least you can pinpoint the date she left London."

"And it's fairly certain she was traveling as Nancy Miller, unless she managed to snag another fake ID and passport somehow."

"Yeah, in that short time, it's doubtful." Ron said he had to go to the courthouse and research something on another case, so I went back into my own office to log in.

By lunch time I'd done it. Nancy Miller had flown from

London to New York on the earliest flight of that Tuesday morning after she texted Graham. From there, I looked for connecting flights, but that was a huge problem. From JFK and the other nearby airports, a person can literally fly to anyplace on the face of the earth where an airplane will take you.

Of course, it was possible she'd stayed in New York. She had connections there, friends and business contacts from her modeling days. I placed a call to Jenna's former agent but wasn't especially surprised when the woman told me she hadn't heard from Jenna since she left New York to get married. I asked about Jenna's friends from those days, but that led nowhere either.

The only other person I could ask about friends from her modeling days was Talbot, and that wasn't happening. We'd already discussed and decided that we would not yet admit to him that we knew Jenna had survived the ocean. Not until we could be a hundred percent sure we could trust him.

I thanked the agent and went on with my search, day by day, airline by airline. When it became apparent she hadn't flown out during the month after her arrival in New York, I gave up in frustration. My back was aching, my neck completely kinked. I hobbled out of my office, mug in hand.

I'd missed lunch, a rarity for me, so I browsed through the office freezer and came up with a Lean Cuisine that I hoped hadn't been in there too long. Nuking it and trading my mug for a tall glass of water, I planned to carry my little meal upstairs, but Ron came in through the back door just then.

"How's it going?"

I think I groaned. "I thought about what Jenna told

her friend Barb, how one day she dreamed of living on an island. So my first searches were for places in the Caribbean, Hawaii, Polynesia."

"Wow. No wonder you look like someth— Never mind."

"You want to help with this?" I threatened to toss the plastic food tray at him. "Then I got to thinking … If Jenna told that dream to her friends, odds are that Talbot also knew about it. So, if she's playing it safe, she'd go somewhere opposite of a tropical island, right?"

"Okay."

"And that's when I ran out of steam and needed food. The non-island world is a big one." I forked up some chicken and rice, too hungry to wait.

"Let me pitch in and help go through the records."

"Thank you." I tried not to let my inner snark creep in. "Where should we start?"

"Iceland?"

This time I grabbed a spoon and really did throw it.

"You take North America and I'll take Asia. If she'd planned to go somewhere in Europe, why fly back to New York first?"

"Okay, that makes sense." I finished the last few bites of my orange chicken and rinsed out the dish. We walked up the stairs together. "I've pretty well covered the month following her return from London. Start with anything after that."

By five o'clock we both agreed we were pretty much spinning our wheels. "Time to go home and get some rest," Ron said, standing in my doorway. "This database will always be here. With a good night's sleep, maybe I'll be thinking a little more creatively."

I had to admit I was feeling entirely frustrated with the case at this point, too. "Maybe we just need to tell Talbot we've exhausted all the options and haven't found her."

"And what about Kiley? You feel some kind of connection with that girl, Charlie. I know you do. You going to just walk away from her needs?"

Okay, he had me there. "Yeah, sleep is what we both need. This will look different in the morning."

I switched off lights, called Freckles to me, and walked out to my Jeep. We walked into the house to find Drake getting ready to grill burgers. I looked at the four patties on the plate. "What's all this?"

"Company's coming. I hope that's okay. Elsa called me over this afternoon when I got home, needing a minor carpentry job done. The two of them just seemed a little down, and we *had* talked about having them over. I thought maybe a little change of scenery would do them some good."

I felt my own exhaustion melting away. Being around someone else, having a completely new conversation, would be good for me too. From the kitchen window I spotted Gram and Dottie walking through the break in the hedge. Dottie had a large bowl in her hands.

"I need to drop off my briefcase and freshen up a little before I talk to anyone," I said, turning toward the living room.

"Don't worry. I've got this."

I scooted off to the bedroom and closed the door as I heard vibrant voices greeting Drake in the kitchen. Pulling my hair into a ponytail, refreshing my lipstick, and changing into a looser t-shirt helped my mood. By the time I emerged, Dottie was setting the dining table for four.

"Hey, girl. You been working too hard, Drake tells us."
She gathered me into a big hug against her pillowy bosom.

"It's that Farber case. Instead of wrapping up, it
seems to be getting more complicated." I waved it off as
we walked into the kitchen. "At this moment I'm more
interested in those burgers."

Drake was on the back porch, tending the gas grill.
Elsa stood in the kitchen, rummaging for a serving spoon
for the potato salad they'd brought.

"We talked about eating outside," she said, "but the
evening's getting a little chilly already."

"The dining room is fine," I assured her.

Drake had already sliced tomatoes and onion, arranged
lettuce leaves on a plate, and pulled four cheese slices from
the pack. I looked around for other accompaniments for
the meal, but the ladies assured me burgers and potato
salad would be plenty. I love simple dinner parties!

"So, what's new in your world?" I asked, once we were
seated at the table.

"Want to hear about our medical appointments?"
Gram asked with a twinkle in her eye. "I didn't think so."

"Drake and I flew up to our little cabin a couple days
ago," I said. "Once we do a decent spring cleaning, we'll all
go. Make a relaxing day of it."

Drake reached for my hand. "Charlie needs a relaxing
day, sometime soon. Did she tell you she's been all over the
place, tracking down this missing woman?"

"Talbot Farber's wife, isn't she?" Gram asked. "Do you
think he did something to her?"

"Maybe she found out about something illegal in his
business dealings. Or maybe he was just tired of being
married," Dottie added.

I set my fork down. "We really don't know at this point. We've discovered some inconsistencies in his story, and there's definitely more to the Farber business enterprises than first appeared."

Dottie sat up straighter in her chair. "I think he pushed her off that ship, for the insurance money."

"If he is involved, he likely didn't act alone," Drake added.

It was the second time today I'd heard the theory about an insurance policy as motive. Talbot certainly hadn't opened that door for us. As the others chatted on, bringing up other possibilities, I let my thoughts free-flow over the various clues we'd discovered.

The implications of Talbot's lies were enormous. I pictured the man Jenna had told Graham about, following her in London, and the menacing guys who always seemed to be near him. If he was directly involved in Jenna's disappearance, as several suggested, then he had been deceiving us from the start. I'd begun to believe we could no longer take anything he said at face value.

Who else might be in on it? His parents, his employees? We were dealing with dangerous, cunning people who had created an elaborate deception.

* * *

We ended the meal with homemade chocolate chip cookies, courtesy of Gram. I was glad when the conversation drifted away from the Farbers and turned toward Gram's plans for her garden this spring. I didn't want others placed in danger by knowing what I knew about this case.

"You seemed a little edgy this evening," Drake said,

after we'd walked our guests to their own back door.

"I guess." We settled on the living room sofa with coffee. "I'm a little cautious about Farber, not knowing how widespread this network of his extends. But we can't let that stop us. I have a feeling Jenna is out there somewhere, maybe scared and probably in danger. I feel like we owe it to her to keep digging."

I took a long sip of my coffee. The implications of what we had uncovered were unnerving, but I also knew we couldn't let emotions cloud our judgment. There were still missing pieces to this puzzle and we needed to stay focused.

"Okay, let's think this through," Drake said. "You've discovered that Jenna was using an alias and traveled a convoluted route to hide her movements. That means she felt threatened or was running from someone."

"Has to be Talbot. The question is, did he do something to her or did she choose to vanish to get away from him?"

"My guess is that something made her fear for her life, to go to such extremes to cover her tracks." Drake set his mug down. "I wonder if it's related to whatever was being delivered to that building out at his ranch?"

I shrugged, thinking back to our interview with Talbot. His polished charm and concern had seemed so convincing at the time. But now we knew he was hiding things. "Talbot's our client, but Ron and I are definitely untrusting of him now."

Drake gave me a long, steady look. "Watch your back, every step of the way."

"I will. We'll find the evidence. We'll find Jenna. And we'll make damn sure we keep her safe." I carried the empty mugs to the kitchen, and on that note we headed for bed.

* * *

I got a call from Ron the next morning, just as Drake and I were finishing breakfast.

"I'll be late getting to the office," he said. "Just wanted to let you know.

"What's up?"

"Joey's got a game this morning, and I'm up for carpool."

Ron's youngest was into softball now and—something I'd lost track of—today was Saturday.

"You want to call me from the field, and we'll talk about our next steps in the investigation?"

"Why don't you meet me there and we can make notes. Otherwise, I'm probably stuck there until well after noon." He gave directions to the ball field complex where today's game would be.

Why not? A morning in the fresh air would do us both good. I gave Freckles the unwelcome news that she needed to stay home in her crate for a while. Grabbing my computer bag, I headed across town to the sports complex off Lomas and I-40.

Ron's Mustang was already there. I found a spot two rows away, where I parked, tucked my laptop safely under the back seat, and locked my doors. I couldn't think of the name of Joey's team, but I did remember their uniforms were turquoise and black. I followed a harried-looking mom with two of those in tow. We came to a small set of bleachers and I spotted Ron on the second tier. He gave me a wave.

The game hadn't started yet, so the crowd was generally milling about, parents carrying lidded coffee cups and fold-up chairs so they could watch from ground level.

"So, you're going in to the office on the weekend?" Ron asked, by way of greeting.

"Yeah, why not? Drake's got maintenance on the aircraft that'll keep him busy at least all morning."

"You can stay here and watch ten-year-olds play ball," he teased.

I gave him a look. There are reasons I don't have kids, and spending my weekends among a crowd of screaming, irate parents is one of them.

"So—the case." He pulled out his little leatherbound notebook.

"Can we get more detail on his financial records, look for any large withdrawals or transfers around the time Jenna disappeared? That might point to payoffs or something shady. Also, the subject of life insurance has come up. If there was a policy on Jenna, it probably wouldn't have paid until she was legally declared dead, so somewhere around seven years after she vanished."

"Good idea," Ron said. He jotted a note. "I'll put in a request first thing Monday."

If my computer hacking skills were better, there was probably a way to get that information without letting anyone know we were looking for it. But since I'm not a hacker, and since Ron wants to keep his PI license, we'd better do this through channels.

"In the meantime, I'll go back to the travel records again. There's got to be a paper trail that shows where she went after New York." As much as I really didn't relish more time in the mind-numbing database, it had to be done.

We each had our assignments, and Ron was all set to start cheering for his son's team, so it seemed an ideal time for me to exit. A latecomer was more than happy to get my parking space when I pulled out and started the drive across the city. Anticipating a long day at the desk again, I stopped at a market along the way and bought a fresh salad for lunch. All set.

Whether the planets were in alignment or I'd curried some favor with the gods of the databases, this time it only took me twenty minutes to score a hit on Nancy Miller's name. Vancouver, BC to Anchorage, Alaska—six weeks after she'd been to London to see Talbot's brother.

Doubting my good luck, I remembered how many Nancy Millers there were in the world, but, since this was an international flight, her passport number was listed on the flight manifest. It matched what we'd found before, for Jenna.

I did a little happy dance around my office, then picked up my phone and called Ron. I could hear shouts and cheers in the background. Giving it a minute for the hubbub to die down, I shared my good news.

Ron had me repeat it. "How did she get to Canada? She have any family or contacts there, or Alaska?"

"No idea on the how. It's not as if these things always have a direct A-B-C connection. Some other mode of transportation, most likely. And contacts—not that we know of. But it's a good place to disappear. Alaska has a lot of islands ..." Although that wasn't exactly what anyone pictured when Jenna described her dream life.

"Wow. Both Canada and Alaska are huge and very spread out."

We were silent for a moment, contemplating our next move. "If we can figure out whether she's still in Anchorage, or where she ended up after that, I want to go and check it out personally."

Chapter 18

What was it about spring—a renewal of life, the promise of green plants once again, the mood of change in nature—that always led her to hold her loved ones nearer to her heart?

She'd thought of them often, this month. Remembering her daughter's soft golden hair, so fine that it refused to stay in barrettes. The smell of baby soap and shampoo, the smear of chocolate around her mouth, from a cookie.

And before that—friends in California, especially those she'd known since elementary school, treasured memories of their good times in high school. She opened her bottom dresser drawer and reached for the square rattan basket stashed under a small lap quilt. She wished the quilt had come from her Grandma Caldwell, the one so talented with needlecrafts, but nothing from those days had survived her ordeal. She had only the memories.

The rattan basket guarded her treasures, the almost-memories. She lifted the lid and stared at the stack of neatly addressed envelopes. Every year—thirteen of them now—she'd chosen a birthday card for her little girl. Every year she addressed the card. Twice, she'd taken them to the post office, only to reverse direction at the last second and not drop the card into the post box.

Common sense told her not to take the chance. She had no idea what had happened back home, but her regular forays into social media and internet news told her that her enemy was still alive and well. And he could very well be looking for her. An envelope might be all it took for him to track her down.

She spread the envelopes out and looked at them, all addressed to her nearest and dearest. Most were unsealed, so she pulled the cards out and reread them, as she did almost every year at some point, either in the spring or at the holidays. They tugged at her heart, and the tears would flow. And then she would put them away again, her emotional slate cleansed for a while longer.

Now, she stuffed the cards back into the basket, stood up, and paced the floor of her small dwelling. When would this end? She berated herself, as she had so many times in the past, for not having enough courage.

Her phone rang, startling her, eliciting a small cry. But when she looked at the screen and recognized a local number, she realized no one from the past could call her here, not even if they wanted to.

She'd done an excellent job of covering her trail and erasing all connections.

Chapter 19

I paced my office, thrilled with the breakthrough I'd discovered, not at all sure what to do with the information. I couldn't very well just head off to Anchorage—although I wanted to—without some kind of plan.

Willing myself to be patient, I went down to the kitchen and retrieved my salad, feeling very righteous because I'd chosen a healthy lunch over my usual fast food burger and fries. I was pouring the dressing over it when I heard the office line ring.

Normally, I would ignore it on a Saturday, and I almost did. But curiosity got the best of me. I walked to Sally's desk and picked it up without even looking at the caller ID. I was probably about to get solicited for an extended warranty on my ten-year-old car.

"Is this RJP Investigations?" asked a female voice.

"Yes, it is." I should have answered properly, the way Sally does. "Are you looking to discuss a new case?"

"Um, no. I think I may have some information. I don't know if this is even important."

At least it wasn't about a car warranty.

"I spoke with a lady from there, a Charlie Parker."

"I'm Charlie."

"Oh! Good. This is Barb Walker, in Pasadena."

My heartbeat picked up immediately. "Yes, Barb. You said you may have some information about Jenna?"

"Well, I don't know if it means anything at all. But I was cleaning out a closet this morning and I came across a stash of old birthday cards I've kept for years. Mostly the mushy ones my husband gives me." Her voice had grown soft, but then she cleared her throat. "Anyway, that's not what you wanted to know. What might be helpful is that I got one from Jenna."

"Okay …"

"But it's not signed and it came after she disappeared."

I was walking back toward the kitchen now, wondering if she would get to the point before my salad wilted. "If it's not signed, how do you know Jenna sent it?"

"I'd know her handwriting anywhere. And she always called me Malibu Barbie, in a teasing way, like I was her favorite Barbie doll or something." There was a short pause. "Inside the card, she wrote 'Hey Malibu, Have a great birthday!'"

I felt a rush of hope, but tempered it. "And you didn't think to tell anyone you'd heard from Jenna after she was lost at sea."

I heard a deep breath, maybe defensiveness. "I didn't know of her disappearance right away. Talbot apparently didn't bother to tell her friends. Sorry. I'm sure he was completely devastated by it, and probably still held hope. I got the card, loved it, put it away with other keepsakes. That's where it's been all this time. After I heard Jenna had died at sea, I just didn't think to go back and look for the card."

"Okay. I apologize for my tone. Can I ask you something else?" And here's where I held my breath. "Did you keep the envelope?"

"Um, yes."

"Does it have a return address?"

"No. Nothing but my name and address."

"What about the postmark—can you tell what city it came from?"

"Let's see ... It's really faint. Starts with an S. I can read S-O-L-D-O-T. There's something more but it fades out."

"That's okay. That helps a lot." I thanked Barb profusely, feeling like fate had been looking out for me today.

She offered to send me a photo of the envelope, an offer I quickly accepted and gave her my email address. Drake and I had worked with the helicopter one summer in Alaska, and I remembered Soldotna as being closer to Anchorage than where we'd been, in Skagway. But this was a terrific lead.

I carried my salad upstairs and forked up lettuce and chicken strips as I dug into my desk drawer for an Alaska aviation map I'd kept. Soldotna was accessible by road from Anchorage, which made it a viable target for Jenna, or Nancy, and it was still somewhat remote if she was looking for a place to disappear.

I became lost in the map, memorizing towns and routes where Jenna might have gone. Now, I could only hope that she'd stayed there and not moved to some other remote corner of the world. I needed to know that, before I went crazy with a travel itinerary to Alaska for myself. I called Ron and asked him to come by the office as soon as he'd dropped the kids off after their game.

Meanwhile, I poked around in his Rolodex—yes, he still has the old-fashioned kind with little cards attached to a wheel—trying to find out whom he went to when he wanted a search of driver's license records. His system for filing is so strange that I was meeting dead ends with everything I could think to try.

Luckily, he came walking in and quizzed me about what I was doing at his desk.

The whole story spilled out, about the random birthday card and the new lead on Jenna's whereabouts. "How do we find out if either Nancy Miller or Jenna Caldwell Farber has an Alaska driver's license?"

He held up an index finger, to say *wait*, while he took over his Rolodex again. Within a minute, he had selected a card and was picking up his phone. The call began with, "Hey Cathy, I need a favor ... yes, on a Saturday, if you can swing it."

I raised an eyebrow at the familiarity, but knew Ron had contacts in practically every nook and cranny in the state.

"Now, we wait," he told me.

I pretended to be meekly going back to my desk, but in truth I spent the next ninety minutes researching flights to Alaska and rental cars in Anchorage. By the time Ron appeared in my doorway, I was ready to hit Book It on my itinerary.

He nodded. "Nancy Miller does have an Alaska driver's license. Try as I might I couldn't get a copy of it without an official police warrant, but my contact was able to say she's the right age."

"Do we have an address for her?"

"Nope. That's what we'd need the search warrant for."

"It's okay. I think if I actually go there and start asking around, I can find her." I clicked the link that finalized the trip.

"Charlie …"

"We'll bill it to Talbot as Miscellaneous Travel Expenses. Same as last time." I cut off his next comment by picking up my computer bag, the map, and my purse. "I'm out of here first thing in the morning."

Chapter 20

An icy wind bit at my cheeks as I stepped out of the terminal in Anchorage. After two weeks of searching, I was finally in Alaska, and I was discovering that spring comes a lot later up here.

"Can I help with your bag, ma'am?" a porter asked. I thanked him and shook my head, slinging my duffle bag over my shoulder.

The rental car keys clinked against their plastic tag as I strode across the parking lot. A light snow had begun to fall, dusting the blue Subaru sedan in white. This was not the forty-five-degree weather I'd been led to believe there would be. I cranked up the heat and followed signs onto the highway, heading southeast on the winding road toward Soldotna.

My hands gripped the wheel tightly. After the weeks

of dead ends and false leads, my gut told me this time was different. Jenna was here in Alaska; I could feel it. Had to be.

The snow picked up, limiting visibility to just a few feet in front of the car. I squinted against the heavy flakes, easing up on the gas. I blew past a sign that said Bridge Ices Before Road, fishtailing slightly on a patch of black ice. Stay focused, Charlie. Eyes on the prize.

As I neared Soldotna, the snow tapered off and I edged my speed upward. The surrounding scenery was beyond gorgeous, with a crystal blue river and towering pine forests. The roads were clear here, for now. As the little town came into view, I eased up on the gas, staying within the speed limit. This was where Jenna had mailed a birthday card, more than twelve years ago, and I found myself hoping like crazy that I would find that she'd stayed here. Now, I just had to figure out how to locate someone who didn't want to be found.

I cruised the length of the town along Alaska Highway 1, passing a visitor center and a few small motels. There was a mall, a couple of antique stores, two major grocery stores, and (no real surprise) a McDonald's and a Starbucks.

Which of these was likely to give me a tip about Jenna, I pondered. Figuring locals didn't often go to the tourist center or stay in a motel, but surely everyone ate out now and then, I looked for a place that looked like it had been here a while and catered to residents.

After two tries where the employees on duty quickly shook their heads at the sight of Jenna's photo, the Mudlark Diner was the next one that seemed to fill the bill—a hole-in-the-wall joint with peeling teal paint and a flickering neon Open sign in the foggy window. I killed the engine on my rental and pocketed the keys, triple-checking that I had Jenna's picture secure in my bag.

A bell jingled above me as I stepped inside. Only two customers sat at the counter—an elderly man in a John Deere cap nursing a coffee, and a guy who, based on his clothing and scent, was probably a fisherman. A middle-aged waitress leaned against the register, her jaw working over a piece of gum. Her name tag identified her as Mary.

I slid onto the stool nearest her and cleared my throat. She turned, sizing me up with sharp brown eyes framed by crow's feet.

"Can I help you?" Her voice was raspy from years of smoking.

I pulled the photo from my bag and set it on the counter. "I'm looking for someone, and I was told she may live here in town."

Mary's gaze dropped to the photo, and her eyes went wide. She snatched it up, hands shaking slightly.

"Nancy," she breathed. "Lord, it's been ages …"

My pulse quickened and I prayed this was the break I'd been waiting for.

"So you do know her?" I pressed gently. "Anything you can tell me would be a huge help."

Mary chewed her lip, staring down at the photo. "Yeah, I know her. Or knew her, I guess. Used to come in here all the time …"

I leaned forward, really wanting this to not be another dead end.

Mary's eyes misted over as she gazed at the photo. "She and my daughter Amber were thick as thieves back then. Nancy would come over to the house, help with Amber's homework. She was so sweet with her."

She sighed, shaking her head. "I can't believe it's been several years. Feels like just yesterday she was out to the house, chatting my ear off."

I nodded, trying not to seem too eager. "When was the last time you saw her?"

"Oh, it's been a while," Mary said. "Maybe a couple years? Amber said she took a job in Anchorage. That's way too far to commute, but I never did get the full story there."

My mind raced.

"So, you think she moved to Anchorage? Any idea where?" I asked.

Mary shook her head and pursed her lips, thinking. "No, I think she's still in the area around here. Amber mentioned a while back she'd heard Nancy was working as a teacher for those homeschool families out in the woods near Kasilof. She might be. Since I started working here at the Mudlark, I don't see hardly anybody that don't eat greasy burgers." She gave a little laugh. "She could be around and we just haven't crossed paths."

I smiled, barely able to contain my excitement. Finally, a real lead after all this time.

"That's incredibly helpful," I said. "Thank you, Mary. I can't tell you how much I appreciate it."

She eyed me curiously. "If you don't mind me asking … why are you trying to find Nancy?"

I hesitated. How much should I reveal?

"Let's just say she left some unfinished business behind. I'm trying to help set things right."

Mary nodded, seeming to accept this. She slid the photo back to me. "Well, I hope you find her. Always did wonder what happened to that girl once my daughter graduated and headed for the lower forty-eight."

I tucked the photo away and slipped off the stool, feeling hopeful.

Out in the rental car, I looked again at the map. Kasilof was the next small town down the road. Surely someone there would recognize Jenna's photo. But what if they warned her someone was looking? She knew the area. I did not.

I drove away from the diner energized with this new lead on Jenna's whereabouts. According to Mary, she was working as a teacher for homeschooling families. Unless she commuted daily, she most likely was living in a remote cabin somewhere near Kasilof. It wasn't much to go on, but it was more than I'd had so far during this search.

As I drove my rental car out of Soldotna toward Kasilof, I tried to imagine what Jenna's life must be like now. The Jenna I'd heard about had been a socialite and model—always dressed to the nines, constantly at parties and charity events on Talbot's arm. That glamorous lifestyle seemed a world away from the Alaskan wilderness.

To disappear so suddenly, and completely reinvent herself, further reinforced Ron's and my supposition that Jenna had learned something about Talbot and his business dealings that made her believe her life was in danger. Even so, she must have believed Kiley was safer to stay behind in Albuquerque. I wasn't sure I understood that, but I'd have to locate Jenna first and see what I could learn.

The further I drove from Soldotna, the more remote the landscape became. I passed towering pines and icy blue lakes. It was staggeringly beautiful, but also isolated. If Jenna wanted to disappear, she couldn't have chosen a better place.

It was getting late when I arrived in Kasilof, and choices

of lodging were limited. Roadside signs gave the idea that the place was known for fishing and hiking. I immediately got the feeling a stranger would be noticed, so I decided to go back to Soldotna and find a room. I would start fresh in the morning and see what more I could uncover by asking around. A good night's rest would help me strategize my next move.

I checked into a motel on the edge of town, anticipation battling fatigue. Tomorrow, hopefully, I would come face to face with the woman I'd been seeking for so long.

After a quick call home to let Drake know I'd arrived safely, and another to Ron to say that I'd gotten a firm lead on Jenna, I gave in to my tired side. A shower lulled me, and the fresh sheets on the bed sent me off to a dreamless sleep.

The next morning, I grabbed a quick breakfast at the Mudlark Diner in town, where a younger waitress was on duty now. The coffee was strong and bracing, just what I needed to sharpen my focus for the day ahead. I had an omelet and toast, and was back in my rental car a half hour later.

Down the road in Kasilof, I pulled in at the small grocery. I love places like this in little towns. Who needs a superstore or a dozen specialty businesses when you can find a little of everything in a place like this? I picked up some tourist brochures and a map, then went to the counter where I added a lip balm and a pack of cinnamon gum to my stack. The clerk was an older woman, dressed in jeans and a heavy flannel shirt.

I asked her if she knew of any women in the area who taught homeschoolers.

"Oh sure, there's Nancy Miller," she said without

hesitation. "She lives maybe two miles outside of town. Keeps to herself mostly, but I've heard she's real good with the kids."

I opened my new map and asked her to point the way, pretending I would be here for the summer and didn't want my kids to fall behind in schoolwork. It was a tricky ploy, yes, but I'm not above such things when I'm set on a goal.

Chapter 21

The sound through her open window, although distant, caught her attention immediately. Living in a place where the quiet was disturbed only by birdsong, the wind in the trees, and the occasion chitter of a small creature, one quickly discovered how intrusive were the sounds of outsiders. She looked up from her crossword puzzle and tilted her head to listen more closely.

Yesterday's snow flurries had given way to rain during the evening hours, a pleasant little drizzle. She'd brought in firewood, checked her food supplies and made a shopping list, and now sat with her mid-morning cup of tea and a crossword. The Peters family, with their two children, aged eight and ten, were expecting her this afternoon for their math lesson. Both kids were bright, personable, and much more interested in helping their dad set rabbit traps than in memorizing multiplication tables. She'd found that putting math problems in terms of nature helped hold their interest. Two robin eggs in each of three nests would equal how many baby robins this spring. That sort of thing.

The mechanical sound caught her attention again.

Not a delivery truck. She knew their sounds, plus she was not expecting anything. This was a passenger car of some kind, if she had to guess. Automatically, she tensed.

She could pretend to not be home. But her vehicle was out front, and the telltale smoke rising from the woodstove chimney would give her away. Plus, she would have to rush about and close the curtains or she would be spotted. She set aside her crossword and stood. The vehicle was definitely coming up the narrow road leading to her place.

She pulled on a lightweight fleece jacket and walked out the front door. From the porch she caught a glimpse of blue metal through the trees. She stepped down to the yard, picking up the ax she'd left at the chopping block.

Chapter 22

I set out in the direction the grocery clerk pointed me, driving slowly on winding dirt roads through dense forest. Aside from a narrow trail here and there, it all looked the same, and I started to worry if I'd ever find the right cabin. But the clerk had told me to take the third driveway off the two-lane track, so I did. Finally, in a small hollow surrounded by trees, I spotted a small cabin.

As I pulled into the clearing, there was no mistaking the woman standing there with a long-handled ax in her hand. I recognized her immediately—the long auburn hair, her face free of makeup now. She wore jeans and a purple fleece jacket. I stepped out of the rental car and smiled.

"Jenna, I'm Charlie—"

The moment I said her name, she flung the ax to the ground and ran. I tossed my purse back into the car and took off after her. She'd disappeared around the side of the cabin. By the time I got there I couldn't see her. But I caught a flash of the purple fleece jacket twenty yards away in the trees. I bolted toward her.

The ground was mushy from the morning rain and my trainers sunk an inch deep. Every step was a struggle, and I didn't even want to look down at them. I kept sight of Jenna, barely.

As a kid, I used to be quite athletic, chasing and rough-housing with my brothers. But that was a lot of years ago. A desk job and avoiding the gym had taken a toll on my fitness level. And Jenna had the advantage—she knew these woods. I had to keep her in sight.

She zigzagged to the left, leaping over a fallen tree trunk. I stumbled on a rock, stifled a curse at the pain in my toe, and kept going.

Come on, Charlie. You don't want to be lost in these woods.

That thought gave me a burst of energy and I began to gain on her a little. Ten yards behind … five now. She heard me and picked up the pace.

"Jenna!" I wheezed. "I'm not going—" I slipped on the uneven ground and she gained some distance again, glancing over her shoulder toward me before running again.

I took advantage of her slight pause and, gauging her path, ducked around the other side of a tree and got close enough to make a grab for her arm.

She spun on me, raking her nails at my face. Luckily, she missed my skin and got a fistful of my shirt at the shoulder. She gave a hard yank, trying to send me into the mud, but I managed to keep my feet.

"Stop it! I've spoken to Kiley!" I shouted.

That took the steam out of her. The moment our eyes

met, she let go of my shirt, breathing heavily.

"Who are you?" she said, her voice barely more than a whisper. She looked exactly as she had on the ship, just older and wearier.

"Charlie Parker. RJP Investigations. I was hired to find you," I said, bending forward to grip my knees and catch my breath.

Jenna glanced around nervously, as if expecting someone else to emerge from the woods.

"You shouldn't be here," she said. "It's not safe."

"Look—I just want to talk. Can we do that? Please?"

Jenna led me back to the small cabin, where she ushered me inside, shutting the door quickly behind us. Her eyes were still darting toward the windows anxiously.

"How did you find me?" she asked.

"Long story, and Soldotna was just the last leg of it." I explained about the photo and the waitress at the diner. Jenna nodded, seeming deflated now that her identity had been discovered.

"Talbot had you legally declared dead seven years after the incident on the ship. Everyone thinks you are. But then he says he saw you in the Denver airport. That's when he hired us to find you."

"Damn, that was such a mistake. But I suppose I knew this day would come eventually," she said with a sigh. She sank down into a chair by the fireplace, motioning for me to sit as well.

"Just tell me—did he push you overboard?"

"Is that what you thought?"

"We'd begun to think he might be capable of it," I admitted.

"No, he didn't do that." Jenna stared into the embers,

gathering her thoughts. When she finally spoke, her voice was strained.

"I witnessed some things in my husband's business dealings, things I should never have seen," she said. "He threatened me, subtly at first, but I knew if I didn't get away, he would …" She trailed off, shuddering. "Well, he actually did—he tried to kill me." She lifted her shirt and showed me a long scar across her ribcage.

"So you staged your disappearance on the cruise?" I asked.

Jenna nodded. "It was the only way I could escape safely. I prepared carefully, used a friend of a distant contact to connect me with someone to set me up with a new identity. I made up a story, saying it was another woman who needed the help. I carried my Nancy Miller documents in a pouch under my clothing, during the whole cruise, waiting for my chance."

"I figured it might be something like that. I discovered your flight from Belize to Atlanta, and I knew you'd gone briefly to London."

Her face paled. "I had no idea it would be so easy to trace me."

"Trust me, it wasn't." I chuckled ruefully about the hours and hours I'd spend combing through the flight manifests online. "And I still have no idea how you got from New York to Vancouver."

She stared toward the front window where my rental car sat. "Bus to Detroit, a car into Montreal, a train across Saskatchewan and Alberta. There was nothing direct about it. I got worried that Talbot might force Graham to admit he'd seen me. I had to be cagey as anything. And since I got here, I've been living very low key. It was all to protect my daughter. As long as Kiley was too young to understand what was going on in Talbot's business, and as long as his parents were there to help keep her feet on the ground … well, I figured she was safer in Albuquerque than taking the chance he would catch me and harm her, out of spite."

She'd begun pacing the room as we talked.

"So … he wasn't mistaken about seeing you in Denver?"

She hung her head. "I was there. I wanted so badly to see Kiley graduate in January, and I took a chance, hoping I would be able to connect with her. She's old enough now to make a choice about where to live."

"It can get complicated, especially if he and his fleet of lawyers want to fight you."

"I know. I haven't set the best example for caring motherhood." Her voice cracked. "I have so many regrets, Charlie." From a side table, she picked up a square basket and handed it to me. "I didn't even have the courage to put her birthday cards in the mail to her. All these years."

I lifted the lid and saw a stack of envelopes addressed to Kiley Farber. I set the basket aside.

"I think that's going to be between you and your daughter. If you come back with me, you'll get the chance to talk to her," I said. "I do have another question. After Denver, did you actually go to Albuquerque?"

She nodded. "I saw Talbot in the Denver airport and I got so scared. I ducked and ran, just dashed out of there and hid in a restroom for more than an hour. Once I'd changed clothes and put my hair up under a cap, I ventured out and rented a car. I drove to Albuquerque and I did get a glimpse of Kiley as she left the house for her graduation. I was too scared to attend the ceremony itself, in case Talbot or his goons spotted me."

"I don't know if they would have been looking. Talbot was pretty shocked at the sight of you in Denver. But still, you were smart to stay out of sight."

"The worst part is, now he knows I'm alive," she said, her voice quavering. "It's only a matter of time before he finds me again."

She buried her face in her hands, sobbing. I sat still, my heart aching for her. The mystery of her disappearance now made perfect, terrible sense.

* * *

I couldn't very well force Jenna to leave with me, especially now that I'd seen her fear and heard more about Talbot's ways. But I didn't want to let her out of my sight until I felt fairly sure she wouldn't just take off and make me chase her down again.

Eventually, she offered tea and a sandwich, and I accepted.

"Do you have cell service out here?" I asked. "I'd like to call my brother—he's my partner at RJP—and let him know what's happened. It seems the most logical thing to do next is that we need to gather evidence of Talbot's crimes and get him put away so he can't harm you."

When I got Ron on the phone, he was in agreement with that approach, but he cautioned me those things can take a long time.

"I'm sure Jenna would love to get back here and see Kiley," he said.

Jenna, hearing him on speaker, nodded. Her eyes had remained teary through most of our conversation this morning. She spoke up. "Can you guarantee my safety if I come back to Albuquerque?"

Ron's silence said it all. We weren't a security guard service.

"I didn't think so," Jenna said. "At this point, Talbot has nothing to lose by killing me. Legally, I'm already dead, right? So all it would take is catching me unaware, making sure my body could never be found. His worries would be over."

I hated the fact that it was so logical. And so true.

"Jenna, I had a thought," I said posing the question to her and Ron at the same time. "Do you have any evidence against your husband, any proof of his illegal activities that the police could use to build a case?"

For the first time since I'd arrived at the cabin, her expression brightened. "I think so. It will depend on how much his business may have changed over the years."

"If we were to find a safehouse where you could stay, would you be willing to fly back with Charlie?" Ron asked. "I'm sure I can get something set up by tomorrow."

I looked toward Jenna and her half-eaten sandwich. She seemed intrigued, especially with the part about putting Talbot away for his crimes. She gave a reluctant nod. I told Ron to go ahead and set the wheels in motion to line up a safehouse.

The call ended and we finished our lunch. "Can I help you pack some things to take along?" I asked.

She looked around the cabin fondly. "I've rented this little place for years now. I'm rather fond of it."

"You don't have to leave it permanently. Maybe Kiley would like to come back here with you."

She gave a wistful smile. "Maybe so."

"Let's do this. Pack enough clothes for a couple weeks.

I'll get us lined up with a flight out of Anchorage. We can drive up there this afternoon and stay in a motel, then catch our flight out tomorrow. By then, Ron will have lodging lined up for you in Albuquerque, and I'll drive you directly there."

She withdrew a little, still scared.

"Once we've got you in a safe place, I'll reach out to Kiley and figure out a way to get the two of you together."

Only the mention of her daughter got Jenna to move. She cleared the plates and headed for the bedroom to pack. I busied myself with a search for flights, and found an Air Alaska itinerary with a short layover in Phoenix, then directly into Albuquerque.

I called out to Jenna, reading off the details. "Does that sound okay to you?"

"That'll work." Her mood seemed lighter than before. The idea that she would soon see her daughter clearly held appeal.

Half an hour later, we were in the rental car, bound for Anchorage. During the nearly three hours together in the car, I went into detail about some of the things we'd learned about Talbot, including the mail drop that appeared to involve making loans to customers.

"I don't know anything about that," she admitted. "Could be a new part of his business. If it's lucrative, he would think of it, so I'm not surprised."

"We turned over the information to the police. It'll be up to them to investigate and find out if what he's doing is actually illegal."

She sighed. "He'll find a way around it. He's got a team of lawyers, and he used to claim they could make anything go away. And another thing—don't believe anything Talbot ever tells you, without some kind of proof. He will spin every single story to his own advantage."

Hm. I was surprised he hadn't gone into politics. Wasn't that their forte? "What about the ranch property near Santa Fe?"

"You found that?"

"Actually took a helicopter flight over the place and got pictures. There was some kind of panel truck outside a large metal building. Ron's trying to run down the identification of the truck and see if we can find out what was being delivered."

"Weapons," she said.

"What?"

"He was getting into that before I left. The man has always been a gun fanatic. In the beginning he just liked to go out to a shooting range for target practice. He took me along. Shooting empty tin cans was kind of fun. Then he figured out how to get a firearms license and started dealing. He once bragged that the big money, though, is not in the legal stuff; it's the bigger weapons that make the most profit."

Now that was a little scary. A man with a hair-trigger temper and a warehouse full of powerful weaponry.

"He's got his own gun range out on the ranch, in a little box canyon area. Used to love going out there to, quote, 'blow stuff up.' I'm assuming he's still doing it."

I didn't recall seeing a formal shooting range on the property, but that didn't mean much. A couple of benches and a few metal targets could easily be stored away when no one was using them. Plus, we hadn't covered nearly all the acreage. We'd probably just missed it.

"Are there weapons at the house, too?"

She nodded emphatically. "He's got an entire secret room, down near the wine cellar. He used to brag that there could be a raid on the place, and you'd never find it unless you knew exactly where to look."

Okay, this did nothing to boost my confidence about getting Kiley out.

"You mentioned having some evidence that could help put Talbot away. Is that something besides what the authorities will find out at the ranch and in this hidden room?"

She nodded, getting quieter as we drove closer to the city.

* * *

I'd booked one room at the Harbor Inn, not wanting to let her out of my sight. The place was cute, with newly painted white wood siding, brilliant blue shutters, and green doors. The whole complex was L shaped, with a parking lot out front. The airport was merely a block away. We checked in and spent most of the evening watching TV. Jenna had become nervous and edgy again, and I had plenty to occupy my mind as I contemplated my responsibilities in getting her home and reunited safely with her daughter. At bedtime, I set the locks and the chain on the door, and even pulled a chair over and wedged it beneath the doorknob.

"That ought to keep us secure for the night," I told her.

With all the excitement of the day, plus tomorrow's plans milling through my brain, I didn't sleep well. As it was becoming daylight, I offered to walk over to the motel office and bring an assortment of the free breakfast items back to the room. Jenna agreed, saying she would take a shower and be ready in ten minutes.

I pocketed my room key and walked to the motel office. Coming back, a few minutes later, I balanced two paper plates, one containing muffins, a couple donuts, and some plain toast, the other piled with scrambled eggs and sausage patties. Walking past the other rooms on the long side of the L, I fished my room key out of my pocket. When it opened, the chain on the inside caught.

"Jenna, come open the chain," I called out. "I've got my hands full."

No response.

"Jenna! Breakfast!"

"Charlie, I'm so sorry. I've changed my mind." I could see her, standing near the bed she'd slept in, pulling on a sweater, her hair damp from the shower.

I pretended not to know what she meant. "If you're not hungry—"

Jenna backed away from the door. "I'm sorry. I can't take this risk."

"Wait! I know you're scared, but—"

A loud thump came from inside the room, followed by the sound of a window sliding open and a rush of air through the four-inch opening in the door. She'd gone out through the tiny bathroom window. Dammit!

I dropped the paper plates and ran to the end of the building, just in time to see a flash of auburn hair and Jenna with her small backpack on, disappearing into the trees behind the motel. I raced after her, but by the time I got to the edge of the thick forest, there was no sign of her.

She was gone again. Cursing under my breath, I hurried

back to the car.

I cruised the streets around the motel—three times. No sign of her. I had been so close to convincing her to come back to Albuquerque. I went back to the room and stuffed things into my bag. Maybe she would have a change of heart and meet me inside the airport terminal.

It was no use dwelling on what-ifs. Jenna was in the wind again, and I had no idea where she might run to next. All I could do now was get myself to my flight on time, back to Albuquerque and hope I could figure out her next moves and pick up her trail.

As the airport came into view, I tried to clear my mind and focus. I needed to figure out what she would do before the woman disappeared for good. I knew she wanted to see her daughter, more than anything. But I had to assume she'd go into hiding somewhere else first, without going back to her little cabin in the woods. She'd already proven her ability to cross an entire continent and not leave a trail.

I sighed in frustration as I pulled into the rental car return lot. I had more questions than answers at this point. But one thing was certain—the clock was ticking. If Jenna made it back to Albuquerque before I could intercept her, there was no telling what might happen.

After turning in the car, I grabbed my carry-on bag from the trunk and hurried into the terminal. I had a plane to catch. I could only hope to find Jenna again before she did something crazy.

Chapter 23

She wanted to trust this Charlie person—she really did. But when it came right down to putting her life in someone else's hands, she had to admit she couldn't do it. Maybe she was just out of practice. But hyper vigilance had kept her alive for thirteen extra years.

When she ran from the motel she took a circuitous route through an industrial neighborhood, hid in a recessed doorway off an alley for thirty minutes, and then found a shop where she could buy a new sim card for her phone. After a couple hours, she figured Charlie had gone ahead to the airport, so she doubled back to the Harbor Inn and picked up her bag. It was not so much that she cared for the clothing she'd packed, but she now knew from experience that a person taking a fairly long trip drew attention if they were traveling with no luggage.

Inside the terminal, she double-checked the monitors to be sure her original flight had left, then approached the ticket counter and pleaded road trip problems coming in from Soldotna as the reason she'd missed the flight. Could they rebook her on a later one?

The agent said she could, and she did. The only problem was that it wouldn't leave for four hours, and the original route through Phoenix was unavailable. Would it be all right to switch planes at Seattle instead?

Perfect, Jenna thought. She used the waiting time to check train and bus schedules.

Chapter 24

I left the jetway and headed through the crowd toward the exits at the Albuquerque Sunport, feeling discouraged that I'd lost Jenna again. I hoped I'd planted enough hope in her heart that she would get to see her daughter again, and maybe she'd relent and come back at some point. I didn't know what else to do, and was just looking forward to going home. I'd sent Ron an email to let him know what happened back in Anchorage; we could talk about it tomorrow.

I'd just stepped onto the downward escalator when a distinctive profile caught my eye. Talbot. He was riding the up-escalator and coming right toward me. Our eyes met.

"Chasing all over the place on my dime, I see," he said with a sneer. "Alaska, huh?"

And then he was past me. I turned to watch him, but

didn't wait for him to get off at the top and come after me. I dodged people and got to the lower level, then ducked into an alcove. How had he guessed where I'd been? We hadn't billed any charges for this trip yet, and we'd certainly not sent him exact itineraries for any of the travel. After three minutes, Talbot had not come back after me.

Without wasting any time, I headed straight for the long-term parking and retrieved my Jeep. My heart was racing as I contemplated how that encounter would have gone if Jenna had been with me. A sick feeling hit the pit of my stomach—Jenna would have believed that I'd told Talbot our plans. That kind of betrayal would have turned her against me forever. For the first time, it hit home that the poor woman really was justified in taking so many precautions.

Still, we needed to find her, mainly to get the evidence she'd told me about, have Talbot put away, and reunite Kiley with her mom.

Although it was getting late in the day, I took the familiar route past downtown, to the Victorian where I knew Ron was waiting for me. I left my bag in the car and went inside. He was at his desk and barely looked up when I walked up the stairs.

"How was your flight?" he asked.

"Well, you already know the worst of it, losing Jenna before I ever got to the Anchorage airport."

He finally met my eyes and nodded. "I know. Rough."

"She could be anywhere by now. I do believe she wants to see Kiley, though. I think she'll come." Then I told him about seeing Talbot a little while ago, and how the man's comments had unnerved me.

Ron's mouth went in a straight line. "He didn't get that from me."

"I know. The part about all the travel could just be a lucky guess. But his mentioning Alaska ... that's scary. I'm just hoping Jenna left there, that she didn't try to go back to her little cabin in the woods."

"One of his acquaintances probably saw you getting off the plane, and that's how he knew," Ron suggested. "Okay, so if Jenna is heading to Albuquerque, there are only so many ways she could get here."

"She admitted to me that she crossed most of Canada by bus and train. She'd likely use something similar to get here, don't you think?"

"One of those, or a rental car. But you have to use a credit card and ID to rent a car. She could probably get a bus or train ticket simply by providing a false name, paying cash, and getting on."

"So we can't track her?"

"I've been checking the schedules. The most reasonable way to do this by train would be for her to first fly to one of the West Coast cities, then ride the train into L.A., or actually, Fullerton, then get on the Southwest Chief, which comes directly here. With a bus, the options are practically endless. But that's a lot slower, especially if she were to take a zigzag route."

"How long does the train take?"

He read off a bunch of times and schedules, but frankly by this time my brain was refusing to absorb more data.

"Bottom line, a little over two days, provided she caught the Coast Starlight right away, there were no major delays, and she didn't get off at any point." He set his reading glasses aside.

"So, we could start monitoring the train station and buses in a couple of days."

"One train a day comes here from the west coast, so that's doable, but with the bus schedules, you're talking about a massive job."

"Okay, I'll take the trains, starting day after tomorrow. You can watch the buses."

He threw a pad of sticky notes at me but I dodged them.

Chapter 25

Jenna stuck a fingernail under the edge of her wig and scratched her itchy scalp. It wasn't the most comfortable way to travel, but wearing a disguise was by far the safest whenever she was within sight of other passengers. She'd paid for a roomette, which at least gave her the privacy of her own space, curtains across the window, and a bathroom. The splurge had severely depleted her cash.

She took a glance in the mirror to be sure the black pixie-cut hair was in place. False eyelashes and bright lipstick served to make her look even less like herself. She gave herself a smile and a thumbs-up. Thank goodness she'd thought to tuck these few items of disguise into the bag she'd packed, back at the cabin. Hard to believe that was two days ago.

She left the safety of her little room and walked to the

dining car. She would eat a light lunch and then step off at the next station and try again to get her crucial phone call to go through. She'd debated about calling Kiley—wanted to speak with her daughter more than anything else in this world—but the danger was too great.

For one, she wasn't a hundred percent convinced that this RJP Investigations was legit or that they weren't still loyal to Talbot. Kiley might say the wrong thing at the wrong moment and Jenna's years of trying to protect them both would be completely wasted.

No, this was better. She picked at her sandwich, a huge thing she had no appetite for, and then made her way to the exit platform as the train pulled into the Klamath Falls station. The new sim card she'd put into her phone had a number with an Alaska area code. Her friend wouldn't recognize it, could very well just choose to ignore the call. And Jenna worried about leaving a voice message. There were so many ways that could go wrong.

She stepped out to the busy platform and found a quiet corner. It was just a quick stop. She wouldn't get a chance to try twice, not until later in the trip.

"Hello…?" Adrienne's voice sounded tentative.

"Rennie, it's me. Don't say my name out loud."

"J—what? Hold on a sec." There were some noises in the background, a door slammed, and then the familiar voice came back. "I had to get to my car. I'm alone. Jen, is that really you?"

"Thank God. I was hoping no one else had adopted the nickname I always used for you."

A laugh at the other end, a sound so dear to her. "No, that was yours alone."

"It's best if you don't use my name or acknowledge that we've talked. I need your help."

Those had always been magic words with Adrienne Hernandez, the most compassionate woman Jenna knew, the person who served on every charity board, helped with every fundraiser. And the only friend who'd spotted Talbot for what he was, smooth on the surface and cruel beneath the veneer.

"Anything." No questions, no need to go into the whole 'what happened to you' scenario. That could come later. For now, there was no hesitation about offering whatever was needed, immediately.

"I'm coming back. It has to be a complete secret. And once I get there, I'll need a car. Something plain that will blend in anywhere." Jenna chuckled. "Kind of ironic, since I used to have a choice of any luxury model I wanted."

"You don't have to explain. When and where do I meet you?"

"I'll have to call you again when I get closer. Another day, day and a half, maybe?"

"I'll work it out."

"When you see me, don't use my real name. Call me ... let's see ... call me by your younger sister's name."

That drew a chuckle. "Okay, Sarah. No prob."

"And Rennie? I know you're super busy, because you always have been ..."

"I'll find a way."

"There's a private investigation firm there in town, RJP Investigations."

"Hire them?"

"No. I just want to check them out—are they legit, good reputation, that kind of thing. But do not reach out to them yet. I'm still figuring out the best way to approach."

"Very good. I can't wait to hear this whole story."

"You will. Gotta go." She hated letting go of the connection, but the conductor was already calling out for boarding. She made her way back to her tiny roomette and collapsed on the short sofa. The tears began to flow.

Chapter 26

Ipulled into the downtown Alvarado Transportation Center parking lot, which was used by both buses and trains, taking in the traditional Spanish mission style building with its adobe-colored stucco and red tile roof. Ron and I had agreed that I'd be here when the Southwest Chief arrived from California. If I had no luck, he would take some alternate shifts and watch the buses.

Inside the stately old station, I checked the schedule and walked out to the platform, peering down the tracks. A Rail Runner train, the daily commuter to and from Santa Fe, was just pulling out. The Amtrak train was due in fifteen minutes. I found a bench inside the station and settled there with a magazine. People continued to filter in, families and friends coming to pick up passengers, a couple of drivers with boards in hand, which they would hold up to catch their clients' attention. I didn't see anyone I recognized.

When the Southwest Chief arrived, the place became a bustle of noise and activity. The doors on all six cars opened at once and people flooded into the station. There were happy shouts and hugs, lunch plans being discussed. The stucco walls and tile floors magnified the sound, excruciatingly. My eyes darted every direction, but I didn't catch sight of Jenna's distinctive hair color, nor anyone traveling alone who looked like her.

In minutes, the station began to empty. It was the only train of the day from the West Coast, and now my third day of striking out. I looked over the bus schedules, but there was nothing coming from the north or west until later in the afternoon. Ron could take that one—I was hungry and grumpy.

Chapter 27

Jenna pulled back from the embrace that felt so good. How long had it been since she'd had a genuine hug from a friend? Still, she kept an eye toward the opposite end of the station where she'd caught a glimpse of Charlie Parker.

"Let's get outside to talk," she told Adrienne.

Her friend pointed to a nondescript little white sedan in the third row of the parking lot and they headed toward it. With her bag in the back and buckled into the seat, she kept an eye on the station doors until they were safely out in traffic on First Street.

"When you called, I'm glad you told me about the black pixie haircut," Adrienne said with a laugh as she steered toward the freeway entrance. "I don't know if I would have recognized you."

"Good! That was definitely the point." Jenna stared out the windows, noting the things about Albuquerque that had remained the same, and the many things that looked different.

They were headed eastbound on I-40 and Adrienne exited at Eubank, then turned north.

"We're going to my place," she explained.

"You've moved?" Jenna remembered an apartment near Coronado Mall.

"Several times. Chad and I split about five years ago, and I found myself the cutest little place." Adrienne glanced at her. "With a lovely guest room that's all set up for you."

Jenna started to protest that she should stay in a hotel but, truthfully, her cash was running low and she wasn't sure if she would raise red flags by using a credit card or accessing an ATM. Everything felt so unsettled, including the tug of emotion that tightened her throat when she thought of Kiley, knowing her daughter was somewhere within a few miles of here.

They cruised into a quiet neighborhood of older homes, and Adrienne pulled into the driveway of a small, gray-stuccoed bungalow, parking beside a shiny SUV in deep blue. Jenna automatically noted that the dealer sticker was not one of Talbot's. A little smile crossed her face.

"Let's get inside," Adrienne said. "I've got salads made for lunch, and then I want to hear everything."

Inside the house, the décor was sleek and up to date. Very Adrienne. Jenna took in the pale gray walls, white plush sofa, vivid pink side chairs, and white bookshelves filled with family photos of people she remembered. A home office kept the same color theme—in here the shelves were filled with plaques and awards for her friend's successful design business.

Jenna felt a rush of pride that Adrienne had obviously stayed with her lifelong dream and built her own business. She thought of where she'd recently been—living in the back woods in a rustic cabin, helping homeschooled kids with their math—and felt a tiny jab of jealousy.

"And here's the guest room" Adrienne said, ushering Jenna into a dreamy room of pale gray and peachy pink, with black accents, and bed linens worthy of a five-star hotel. "Adjoining bathroom, right there. Take as long as you like to settle in. Lunch is in fifteen minutes."

Jenna laughed. "I think I can settle quite well in fifteen minutes."

* * *

She walked into the kitchen to see that Adrienne had the same flair with the luncheon setup that was evident throughout the house.

"You're just too good to me," she exclaimed as they took seats at the small kitchen table.

Adrienne gave her a long look. "Girl, after what you've been through, I'm not sure there's such a thing as 'too good' for you. I want you to rest, recover, and practice some real self-care."

"If those bath products are actually for use, not decoration, I definitely will." Jenna took the first bite of her chicken-cranberry salad. "I need to know—did you get a chance to look into that private investigation firm I mentioned?"

"I did, and they are completely legit. They've actually been involved in a few high-profile cases in the past and came out looking really good. It's a small firm. Ron Parker is the licensed PI, and his sister Charlotte, um, Charlie is the accountant. She also helps a lot with the footwork and travel. And they both have good contacts within the police department. I put out feelers with some friends, and based on the feedback I'd trust them."

"Good. I feel kind of bad now, I ditched Charlie because I wasn't sure of her."

"Hey, better safe than sorry." Adrienne's expression turned sober. "I was so scared for you. So sad when the news said you were gone."

"Tell me about that. I only got a quick glimpse at one newspaper in Belize."

"Well, at first it seemed like they were looking at Talbot pretty closely. Someone goes overboard off a ship, they're going to suspect the spouse. But he played it well. Expressed concern for the families of the other people who'd gone into the water, and kept talking like he just wanted you back home, putting out pleas for anyone who might have helped and taken you in. There were interviews with local authorities and coast guard, and after several days it seemed all hope was lost. He had a memorial service for you. I went. His tears seemed genuine enough."

"I'm sure they were. Who was he going to abuse, with me gone?" Jenna took a long sip of her iced tea. "Sorry. I shouldn't make remarks like that."

"Honey, did you … Did you set up your own escape?"

Jenna nodded.

"That was a huge risk. You could have easily drowned."

"I know. I guess I'd been traumatized for so long that I wasn't thinking clearly. Or, dying just seemed preferable to going on." A tear leaked from one eye and she dabbed it with her napkin. She took a deep breath. "But there was Kiley. The whole time I was in the water with my eyes on the lights on shore, I kept picturing her little face, working out a plan to come back for her. It was only after I was back on dry land that I realized how unrealistic I'd been, thinking I could waltz back in and get my child out of his clutches."

She almost said more. But the memory of the phone call intruded, the words she'd overheard between Talbot and one of his political contacts, the final night she'd been aboard the ship. He'd spotted her in the mirror, and she knew she would not live to finish the cruise anyway. It was the whole reason she'd pulled out her emergency funds and identification and set her plan in motion. Creating chaos with the fire alarm, the ship-wide alert, her lightweight clothing that wouldn't pull her under, knowing the ship was as close to shore as it would be all night.

She'd been incredibly lucky with the timing.

Adrienne reached across the table and took her hand. "You poor thing. I'll help you, in any way that I can."

"You already have. A place to sleep for a few days, a car to get around town. I owe you, big time."

Adrienne shook her head. "No, you don't. But there is one thing I want you to do."

Jenna met her eyes, questioning.

"Take a nap after lunch. I have a feeling you haven't had a good night's sleep in a while."

Chapter 28

Two days had passed, and I had a strong feeling Jenna had made it to Albuquerque. If she ever intended to come here, it would be now. And, somehow, she would reach out to Kiley either to patch things up between them or to get her daughter as far from here as she could. Jenna had demonstrated that she was quick and resourceful, so I felt the need to stay on top of this.

Ron caught me pacing in my office. "I gave up on the buses, you know. There are too many, coming from too many cities. I offered the guy at the newsstand a reward if he spotted Jenna and was able to keep her busy while he called me."

"And I guess that hasn't panned out?"

"I didn't hold a lot of hope." He glanced at my beaten-down carpet. "And what are you working on right now?"

"Deciding what to do next. Ever since I saw Talbot at the airport, it's been nagging at me that this might be a good time to talk to Kiley alone."

"And maybe catch Jenna trying to reach her daughter."

"And maybe *help* Jenna and Kiley reunite. I don't think that's going to be an easy scenario for either of them."

He nodded agreement. "She won't take the chance if Talbot's around."

"How can we find out if he's in town?" I asked.

"I'll try calling, make up some excuse to see if he can meet today. If he's not in town, he'll tell me."

Good. I liked that plan better than me trying to call the man. He'd sent unfriendly vibes my way, and I must say the feeling was entirely mutual.

Ron disappeared into his own office and came back a minute later. "He's not picking up. I left a voicemail."

Which could mean anything. "I'm going to drive out there, see if I can catch Kiley alone."

I headed straight for the Farber home, realizing as I approached that it wasn't an easy place for a stakeout. The long driveway, the garage doors that didn't face the road, the imposing mansion that seemed to simply stare at me—none of it revealed what was going on inside.

Okay, Charlie, quit being a wuss. Just drive up there and find out who's home.

I parked in the turnaround at the front and walked up the steps. The front door creaked open and Kiley's head peeked out. "Oh, hey Charlie. What's up? Do you have news about my mom?"

Her question answered mine—obviously she'd not heard from Jenna directly. I gave a rueful smile and shook my head. I'd run through this a dozen times in my head, whether to admit to Kiley that we knew her mother was alive. Until I had Jenna here, ready to meet her daughter, the only possible outcome would be that Kiley's excitement would show and she'd reveal something to her dad that we didn't want him knowing yet.

So, I changed tactic. "Is your dad home? We tried to call and he doesn't answer."

Kiley shifted her weight between feet. "Um, no, he had to go out of town for a business meeting."

"Do you know when he'll be back?"

"Not sure. You know how he is," she said with a shrug.

I nodded, but my gut told me she wasn't being totally upfront.

"Kiley, are you *sure* you don't know anything about where your dad went?" I asked, watching her closely.

She avoided meeting my eyes as she stepped outside and sat on the top porch step. "Well, um ..." she hesitated, biting her lip.

I waited.

"I did hear him talking to Senator Gallegos the other day," she finally admitted.

"What were they talking about?"

Kiley shrugged again. "I'm not sure, I only overheard them for a minute. But he said he had to go meet the senator in New York about some deal they were working on."

I digested this new information. Gallegos was big time in Santa Fe and Washington, head of a couple of important Senate committees. Scuttlebutt was that his reputation was not exactly squeaky clean, but he did get things done for his biggest campaign donors. I could easily imagine Talbot as a big enough donor he could demand favors in return.

She hesitated, then spoke again. "I didn't want you to think badly of my dad. I know he comes off as kind of cold, but he's not a bad person."

I nodded encouragement, waiting for her to go on.

"Senator Gallegos helps fund Dad's business ventures sometimes. Dad didn't want me to tell anyone that." She took a shaky breath. "Please don't tell my dad I told you," Kiley added quickly. "He doesn't like me getting involved in his stuff."

"I won't say anything." I sat down next to her. "Thank you for telling me. Don't worry, your secret is safe with me. And Kiley? If you should hear from your mom, would you please call or text me right away?"

Her face lit up as she nodded. "So she *is* still alive? Do you know where?"

I took a deep breath. "We know she survived the disaster on the cruise ship. We're working on finding out what happened after that, where she might have gone, and where she might be now. But, truthfully, I don't know that, at this point. If we can find her, the goal is to get you two together."

A tiny sob escaped her. I reached over and squeezed her arm before I stood up. "We'll figure this out. And, Kiley? I really need for you not to tell anyone—not even your family—what I've just told you. It's important that we keep your mother's secret until we have a chance to talk with her."

She nodded.

"Promise me. Can you keep the secret?"

"I can. I know, many things could have happened in the meantime. I don't want to get my hopes up too much."

A minivan had turned off the road and was making

its way up the driveway. Kiley stood, turning back to the house. "That's my grandparents. I'm going over to their house until my dad gets home." She reached inside the front door and brought out a small backpack.

"Remember what we just talked about. Not even the grandparents can know anything about your mom, not yet."

She gave me a solemn look and nodded again.

The minivan swung into the turnaround in front of the house, and a couple in their mid-sixties stared through the windshield at me. I stepped forward, quickly deciding my story, as they stopped and got out. Both wore what I would call conservative-expensive, as people with money tended to do. Nothing ostentatious, and certainly nothing from Walmart.

"Hi, you must be the Farbers? I'm Charlie Parker."

The woman took the lead. She set her Coach bag on the passenger seat of the vehicle and reached out to shake my hand. Even I recognized the Patek Philippe on her wrist. "Yes, Grace and Mitch. We're Kiley's grandparents."

I gave my widest smile and half-turned toward Kiley. "She told me. She says her dad's out of town and she's staying with you."

Mitch Farber directed a questioning stare in my direction. Who on earth was I?

"My company is doing some work for Talbot, and I'd just popped by to get some additional information from him. Should have called ahead, I suppose."

Kiley sent me a final smile as she opened the side door on the van. I sent a little wave toward her and hoped like crazy that she really would keep the knowledge of Jenna's survival to herself. I bade the group goodbye and got into my Jeep. The elder Farbers followed me down the long driveway as we all left the property.

My mind switched back to the new information about Talbot meeting with Senator Gallegos, as I drove home, and I felt my mood darkening. The man's sphere of influence and corruption was growing bigger by the minute.

Chapter 29

Like most of their fights, this one began late in the evening. The housekeeper had been there early in the day, but she left at five. Jenna cooked his favorite dinner, beaming when he complimented her on the tenderness of the steak. Two-year-old Kiley was tucked in, a story read, her innocence so touching when Jenna bent to kiss her goodnight.

She walked downstairs, to the richly paneled den, where her husband was watching a tense movie involving a successful Wall Street tycoon. He chuckled when the man fired his loyal secretary. Jenna picked up a novel and walked back to the kitchen for a glass of water.

At once, he was behind her, shouting obscenities, calling her shameful names—something to do with the risqué cover of the book in her hand. She spun around, startled.

"What—"

"You *know* what! You *know* …" And then he had a knife in his hand, one he'd pulled from the block on the countertop.

"Talbot, what are you doing?"

And in a flash, he swiped the blade across the space between them. It sliced through her favorite silk blouse. For a moment there was no pain. Then blood flowed down her side and into her shoe. And the pain came, as if her body—from ribcage to belly—was on fire. She screamed.

He stared at her, shocked, perhaps thinking to threaten her, not realizing he was close enough to actually strike.

The blood continued to flow and she screamed for help. Help that would not come.

"Jenna!" It was Adrienne's voice. "Honey, wake up. You're having a terrible dream."

Jenna's eyes came open slowly, and she realized she was safe in her friend's guest room. Late afternoon sun came through the windows, and Adrienne had gathered her into a hug.

"Wow, that must have been a scary one," Adrienne said, dabbing sweat from Jenna's forehead with a tissue. "It's okay. You're okay now."

Jenna mumbled something about water, anything as a distraction from the vivid recollection, anything to keep from having to answer questions.

"Let me make us a cup of tea. Come on into the kitchen whenever you're ready."

Jenna blew out her pent-up breath, still a bit dazed that the recurring nightmare had come now. She'd not experienced this one in years. Something about being back in Albuquerque had reawakened too many past memories.

She scrubbed at her face with her hands and raked her long hair out of her eyes.

If she'd had a kindly thought toward her husband in recent days, it was gone now. She felt a wave of gratitude. The dream had served to remind her that he'd harmed her before and he would never change. She stood on shaky legs, stretching to gain strength in them.

From the kitchen, she heard the whistle of a tea kettle. She walked in to find Adrienne pulling an assortment of teabags from a canister.

"I need to see Kiley," Jenna announced. "I need to know she's all right, and I need to finally tell her my side of things."

Adrienne froze for a moment, then set the canister down. "Jen, you really need to think about this rather than just waltzing in. What if he's there? What if he's poisoned Kiley's mind against you?"

Both of those were distinct possibilities.

"Jenna, you had me look into this investigator he hired. What's going on with that?"

"I met her. Charlie, the partner at the company. She tried to bring me back to Kiley, but I was afraid."

"Okay, so that's a good start. Did you get the idea you were going to be returned to Talbot?"

"No, not at all. She told me they'd begun to doubt him as a client and she wanted to help me."

"Did you sense deception from her?"

Jenna shook her head.

"Let's look for a way to have these investigators do the confrontation, let them get Kiley back for you, rather than putting yourself in danger again." Adrienne poured the boiling water and handed Jenna a mug.

"They'll need evidence, proof of Talbot's crimes that will put him away. It's the only way Kiley and I will be safe from him." Jenna absently dunked her teabag until the brew was as dark as coffee.

"And what would that be—this proof?"

Jenna chewed at her lower lip for a moment. "After the knife incident I began to make copies of things …"

Adrienne started at the mention of a knife, but she didn't interrupt.

"Documents and papers. There was some kind of a book or register …" She looked up, her eyes bright again. "And you have the key."

Adrienne pointed to her own chest. "Me? What are you—" Recognition dawned. "Literally, a key. You gave me a key to a safe deposit box and told me to keep it."

Jenna nodded vigorously.

"I did. I kept it. Let me think a second." Adrienne set her mug down and rushed out of the room. In under a minute she was back, a tiny paper envelope in her hand. "I put it in my office safe and forgot all about it. What was I supposed to do with this?"

Jenna held out her hand, knowing this was it. "Nothing. Until now."

She looked into the little envelope and saw the special, flat-shaped key. Now, if only the contents were still there. The evidence she'd risked everything to gather.

"The bank closes in thirty minutes. Let's go."

Chapter 30

I drove home, my mind spinning. Kiley's revelation about her father's connection to Senator Gallegos was troubling, but it didn't necessarily mean Talbot was guilty of anything more than the shady business deals we already suspected. Still, something didn't sit right with me.

I checked in with Ron, but he'd not heard from our client either. I hung up, frustrated. Why wasn't Talbot returning our calls?

My phone buzzed with an incoming text. It was from Kiley.

I'm sorry I didn't tell you everything earlier. I'm worried about my dad. He hasn't been answering his phone. This isn't like him.

I stared at the message, my unease growing. Talbot off the grid, right after his wife goes missing again? It couldn't be a coincidence.

Someone was lying to me. But who? Kiley seemed genuinely concerned for her father, despite protecting him earlier. Was Talbot *in* trouble or *causing* it? And where did Jenna fit into all this? She hadn't exactly been easy to deal with either.

I had to get to the bottom of it, and fast, before someone else disappeared.

I paced my living room, thoughts racing about Kiley's text and this sudden new information. Was she covering for him? Or, had she heard from Jenna and didn't want to tell me?

My phone rang, interrupting my speculation. The caller ID read "Ron Parker." I answered quickly.

"Hey, what's up?"

My brother's voice came through, all business. "Just checking in. Was Talbot back home yet? Did you see Kiley?"

I filled him in on what Kiley had told me about Gallegos and the connection with Talbot.

"Hmm," he said. "Something's off here. Why would they meet in New York? Gallegos spends a fair amount of time in New Mexico. Or, it seems Talbot would travel to DC to meet with him at his offices there. I can make some calls, see if anyone has contacts out there we can leverage."

Leave it to Ron to think strategically. "That's a good idea. In the meantime, I'm going to see if I can get a line on Jenna's whereabouts."

We'd no sooner hung up than my phone rang. I didn't recognize the number on the readout.

"Charlie, it's me. Unless you're alone, don't say my name."

"Jenna ... Where are you?"

"I'm at a friend's house. In Albuquerque."

I wanted to lecture, to demand to know why she'd run off. Then I remembered the unfortunate timing when Talbot had passed me in the airport. I took a deep breath—everything had worked out all right, so far.

"Have you tried to reach out to Kiley yet?"

"I ... No, not yet. I'm a little nervous about that. And I need to do something else first."

"What's that?"

"I need to get into the house. He'll have documents in his office or on his computer. Before I try to get Kiley away from him, I want to have the proof in my hands."

"Jenna, slow down a little. We believe Talbot is into several kinds of illegal activities. Is it that? Do you know how to get proof of those things?"

"Yes! Loan sharking—there was a handwritten ledger he kept. I cut several pages from it. I have them. I've got documents I printed from his computer before I left, receipts for weapons he used to buy, communications about money laundering."

"You still—How?"

She went into a story about a safe deposit box at a local bank, and a friend who'd kept the key for her. They'd been to the bank this afternoon and verified everything was there.

"I want to get all of this into the hands of the police. But it has to be someone trustworthy, someone Talbot doesn't have on his payroll."

Like Senator Gallegos, I thought.

"I know someone, several reliable contacts within APD. We'll get that part of it taken care of." I paused in my pacing. "Jenna, isn't the evidence you have enough? Do you really need to get into the house?"

There was a sigh. "What I have is all old material. If

there isn't proof he's still doing the same things, the statute of limitations may have run out."

She had a point. Better to approach law enforcement with present-day crimes. The older material would be useful to prove a history, that his ventures were long-term. The little angel on my shoulder said I should take Jenna and her evidence straight to the police, let them issue a search warrant, and follow procedure.

"Charlie, I'm calling to see if you want to come along with me. I'm doing this, no matter what."

"When?"

"As soon as I can be sure he won't be there, won't catch me."

Okay, my devil side won out. "He's in New York right now, and Kiley is with her grandparents. I saw them leave this afternoon."

"I just want to get into his home office. I know the combination to the safe, and he never was imaginative when it came to computer passwords."

"What about household staff? How many people are likely to be around?"

"Unless he's had a personality transplant, I'd say there will be none. Talbot was always so paranoid he didn't allow anyone other than a daytime cleaning lady. His goons only visited when he was there. No one lives on premises."

That was good news.

"What about getting inside? Do we need lockpicking tools?"

"I know where he always kept a spare key."

There were so many factors and Talbot was probably smart enough to change all of those—from the safe combination to the hideaway key.

"Okay, I'll come. But, if anything goes sideways, anything at all, we are out of there. Immediately."

Chapter 31

It was already getting dark by the time I got off the phone. I changed into a black shirt and retrieved my pistol from the closet. I've never had to use it—have only drawn down on a human one other time—but it does make me feel more secure, knowing I've practiced with it a lot and know how to use it.

We'd agreed to meet at the Flying Star, a popular restaurant a few miles down the road from Talbot's home. I assumed Jenna would borrow her friend's car in order to get there, but I had no idea what to watch for. There was no way Jenna would want to go inside the eatery—too much chance of running into someone she knew from her old life. I parked my Jeep at one end of the crowded lot and sat there, waiting.

Only a few minutes passed before there was a tap on

my window. Jenna bent to study my face, making sure it was me. She'd pulled her long hair up and wore a dark ballcap to shield her face. She'd dressed in dark clothing and had a small pack strapped around her waist. I signaled for her to get in the passenger seat.

"I hope he didn't change the alarm code," she said as she buckled her seatbelt.

"Hopefully, we don't need to find out. I'm pretty sure Kiley didn't set an alarm when she left with her grandparents."

"You were there? How did they look? How's Kiley?"

We let that thread carry the conversation as we headed north along the mostly rural boulevard. I spotted the turn to the house but drove past it, noting a few lights on but no vehicles.

"We always kept lamps on timers," Jenna explained as I parked down the road a short way, choosing a spot with a lot of brush.

"But no staff. You're sure?" I stared at the huge mansion as we entered the property on foot, keeping to the edges where the neatly trimmed shrubs acted as cover.

"As sure as I can be," she admitted. "He never wanted any live-ins. That would have provided an audience for his abusive moods."

"Do you think he's abusive with Kiley?"

"He never was … I was always his target at home. In the dealerships, it was the subordinates, those low enough in the pecking order that he held power over them. He picked on the employees who couldn't afford to quit their jobs."

I thought of Kiley again, a kid who couldn't very well just walk out. And teens weren't the easiest to live with. I remembered myself at that age and marveled that Gram had put up with me. I prayed that Talbot hadn't turned his ugly moods toward his daughter.

"What's your plan?" I asked as we approached the mansion.

Jenna led the way around the side of the four-bay garage and switched on a tiny light imbedded in the bill of her cap. *Note to self: I need to get one of those!* Within a few seconds she'd led the way to an electrical box mounted on the wall. Feeling the underside of it, she withdrew a magnetic key holder and pulled out two keys.

"Once we're inside, we'll check the alarm and hope he hasn't changed the code, in case Kiley has been back and set it. After we take care of that, I need the evidence from Talbot's study." Jenna checked her watch anxiously.

I followed along, realizing if anyone could find a way in there, it was Jenna. She was risking everything to take Talbot down. I felt a surge of admiration for her courage.

The huge house loomed beside us as we made our way around to the front door. Although it wasn't clearly visible from the road, this is where I felt the most vulnerable. My neck muscles tensed, unsure what we would find inside.

The key operated smoothly in the heavy front door, which swung open soundlessly. While I slipped on a pair of latex gloves, Jenna turned to the right and stared at the security system panel.

"Green light," she said. "We're good."

I exhaled and felt a little of the tension leave me.

She locked the front door and started directly down a hall beside the staircase, heading for Talbot's study. I followed along, peeking into other rooms along the way. Soft lamplight illuminated the living room and kitchen, and there was a light at the stairway landing.

In the study, she crossed directly to a wood-paneled wall and pressed some concealed spot about three feet above the floor. One long panel slid aside, revealing a safe about six feet tall and three feet wide. I glanced around the room, looking for hidden cameras or other monitoring devices. I didn't spot any, but wasn't that the point in calling them *hidden*.

A series of electronic beeps sounded as Jenna pressed keys on the numeric pad. Five short beeps, then a long one.

"Well, that wasn't it. He's changed the combination."

I really hoped our trip wasn't going to be a bust.

"He used my birthday. Guess he didn't like that anymore. I'll try Kiley's."

And that time, after the six short beeps, a chipper series of quick ones let us know it was a success.

"As I said, he never was the most imaginative," she said, swinging the safe door open. "Holy cow!"

I had to mirror that sentiment. The whole lower two-thirds of the space was stacked with neatly banded cash.

"I have to say, I'm tempted," she admitted. "Living on gig jobs and a credit card backed by no credit score … it's been …"

She cleared her throat and turned her attention to the upper section of the safe, where three flat drawers held documents. From the top one she pulled out a leatherbound ledger book. The wide pages held nothing but columns of numbers and letters, in no particular order that I could figure out, a code of some kind.

"He still has this old thing. It's the one I cut some pages out of." Thumbing to the back, she explained that the coded dates were very much current.

"What's the ledger for?"

"Records of payments. He makes loans to people who can't qualify for a car loan, then uses a mail drop to receive the payments."

Pretty much what we'd already guessed. "Are the payments ever made in cash?" I asked with a nod toward the stash, which had to total close to a million dollars.

"Not *that* much cash," she said. "I think there's more to it."

"We'd better hurry this up a little. Is there anything here you need to make a copy of?" I'd already pulled out my phone and snapped several photos of the interior of the safe.

She set out four thick file folders and the ledger. "Get as many pictures as you can while I check out the computer."

A sleek new desktop computer held center stage on the desk, and Jenna took a minute to study it. "It's not the one he used to have, but how difficult can it be to plug in a separate drive and copy stuff?"

She pulled an external hard drive device from her waist pack and found a USB port on the computer. With a few clicks she'd started the process.

"I'm just copying the entire documents folder and a few that seem business related. I'd bet he's running the loans and some of the other stuff through the dealerships."

"We found several other corporations in his name," I told her.

"Oh, yeah … I remember." She keyed in the names. "He's got separate folders for each of them, plus one called Operation FunGun."

"Copy those, if your disk has space. It's likely where any information about the weapons imports would be stored."

"Got it."

I put the files back in the safe, neatly stacking them, hoping he wouldn't notice they'd been moved. Jenna came over and closed the safe door and the concealing panel, using the hem of her sweater to wipe her prints from every surface she'd touched. I had to give her credit for knowing how to operate stealthily.

The computer screen showed the progress of the copying process—a little more than halfway there. I looked up to see Jenna standing by the door to the hall.

"Before I leave here, I need to see Kiley's room. I just—" Her voice broke.

"I'll keep an eye on this," I told her with a nod to the computer.

Ten minutes went by, feeling like ten hours as my pulse raced. The longer we were in this house, the more dangerous it felt. When the files finished backing up, I ejected the drive, pulled the plug, and turned everything off. I rechecked the room once more, making sure it looked as we had found it, closing the door behind me.

I found Jenna in the kitchen, tears running down her face.

"This is all too much for you," I said. "Forget about the other hidden evidence you mentioned. Come on, let's go."

She held a pale blue sweater in her hands, caressing the wool. "This was always Kiley's favorite color. As a little girl, she would choose this blue whenever I let her pick out clothes at the store."

"Jenna, we should—"

Her eyes trailed across the kitchen counters, taking in the familiar items. She stepped over to the stove and pulled a knife from the set in a wooden block. Nodding, she whispered to herself. "This is the one."

For a moment I thought she was going to throw the knife across the room, most likely to stick it in a photo of Talbot that was attached by magnets to the fridge. But she turned back and placed it into its slot again.

"What one?" I had to ask.

She rubbed a hand across her ribcage and I remembered the long scar I'd seen there.

"He did that to you? With a kitchen knife?" I felt my ire rising. "We have to go to the police. Right now."

Panic flashed in Jenna's eyes. "No! Talbot has connections everywhere. He'll find out I'm back. He'll …" She trailed off, fresh terror on her face.

My mind raced. Talbot's web of corruption ran deeper than I'd imagined. But if we moved carefully, strategically, we could take him down for good.

"Let's think this through. Jenna, I know you're scared, but we have solid evidence now. Enough to implicate Talbot and take away his power," I said reassuringly.

Jenna lifted her head, eyes glistening. "You really think so?"

"I do. With the documents you found, the police can build an airtight case." I put a hand on her shoulder. "But we need to act fast, before he realizes what we've done. We've got copies of documents, but you also mentioned some physical evidence, something hidden here in the house?"

"Yes—there's a secret room at the back of the wine cellar."

This house held more secrets than the Vatican, I'd swear.

She led the way to a door at the far end of the kitchen. Behind it, a set of stairs went down to a basement. Flipping on a light, Jenna went first. At the bottom we came to a metal gate, behind which I could see rows of wine bottles in racks. Jenna fished in her pocket and came out with the two keys she'd removed from the hide-a-key box. The smaller one opened the gate to the wine cellar.

She walked confidently past the racks of wine and approached the back wall of the small room, which had rock walls and an ambiance like what I'd expect in a castle. A table stood there with a complex-looking wine opener mounted to the surface. Beside it hung a short towel bar with a pristine white towel on it.

Jenna reached under the edge of the table, felt around, and came out with a silver key. Lifting the white towel, she found a tiny lock, almost invisible in the rock surface of the wall. A quarter turn, a click, and the whole wall swung inward. She reached for a string and pulled, illuminating the space.

It wasn't large—maybe four feet square. But the amazing thing were the gun racks covering all three walls. I felt pretty sure most of these automatic weapons were not legal to own. The hair on the back of my neck rose.

"There are even more than when I last saw it," she whispered.

"Okay, let's back out of here right now. First, we need to get those documents somewhere safe. Then we'll contact our buddies in law enforcement. It's time for them to take over."

"You're right. Let's just go," she said, closing the door and replacing the little silver key. We rushed from the cellar and headed toward the front door.

But before she opened it, lights flashed across the front windows. Headlights.

Oh shit.

Chapter 32

I ran into the dining room and peered around the edge of the drapes. "That's Talbot's car!"

"Ohmygod, ohmygod. I thought you said he was in New York." Her face blanched and she seemed frozen in place.

Come on, girl, don't lose your cool now. I grabbed her hand and pulled her through to the back of the house.

"Obviously, he's back. Go! Go!" I whispered. "Stay out of sight. Get down the road to my Jeep. I'm right behind you."

I gave a little shove to get her started. I didn't want to admit that a crazy plan had come to me.

I would be the bait.

I watched Jenna disappear into the shrubbery, heading in the general direction of the road. At least I could attest from experience that she was good at fleeing through wooded places. I scanned the perimeter of the property, willing my heartbeat to slow down and my breathing to be less ragged as I walked slowly toward the front of the house.

The slam of a heavy car door told me he had stopped at the front door. Not the garages—interesting. I walked through the damp grass until I stood in the headlights of the luxury SUV he drove.

The look on his face was priceless. "What are you doing here, Ms. Parker?"

"Hello, Talbot." I so badly wanted to accuse him outright, to blast him with all I knew about his crooked business deals, and how he'd driven Jenna to risk her life to get away from him. But that would be suicidal. "I was hoping to see Kiley for a minute. When no one answered the doorbell, I thought you might be around back. Nice infinity pool, by the way."

"At nine o'clock at night?"

"Teens tend to stay up a lot later than this."

"Cut the bullshit, Charlie. Where's Jenna?"

"At this moment, I really don't know." I kept edging around to give myself a clear run at the driveway—if it should come to that—while keeping Talbot's back turned to the side of the property where, I hoped, Jenna had already made her break for it. I hated to think of her trapped, with nowhere to run.

He turned toward the front door, his polished leather shoes clicking steadily up the front steps, a subtle way of placing himself on higher ground.

"But you did find her, didn't you? She didn't really die all those years ago. Was I right when I spotted her in Denver?"

I shrugged, not about to give him the satisfaction of being right about anything.

"What? Did she tell you I threw her overboard? Because that's absolutely not true."

I sensed desperation creeping into his voice. This was not the time to antagonize him any further. I really didn't want to pull my pistol from the back of my waistband at this point. "No, actually she never said anything like that."

My hand closed over the hard drive in my pocket. "It's over, Talbot. Let Jenna go, and let Kiley be with her mother."

Talbot's lip curled in a sneer, but I thought I detected a flash of fear in his eyes. "Walk away now, girl," he hissed. "Before you get hurt."

He took another step toward the edge of the porch. My fingers tightened. I held Talbot's gaze. I had to keep him talking, buy some time for Jenna to escape.

"Why did you hire us?" I asked, amazed at how steady my voice sounded. "Was it just to be certain Jenna was still alive? Or to send someone out to get rid of her, once and for all?"

Talbot let out a harsh bark of laughter. "You think you know everything, don't you? Just a nosy young woman meddling in things too big for her."

He took another step toward me, but I stood my ground.

"Kiley deserved the truth," I said. "You took her mother from her."

I thought I saw a smirk cross Talbot's face at the mention of his daughter. For just a moment, his icy demeanor cracked.

"You know nothing about it," he said, his voice quieter now. "Nothing about what we had, or how it ended."

My mind raced. Was he actually opening up to me? I had to keep him talking.

"Then tell me," I said gently. "Help me understand."

Talbot looked at me, and I was surprised to see his eyes glistening. When he spoke again, his voice was thick with emotion.

"I loved Jenna more than anything. I never meant to…" He trailed off, passing a trembling hand over his eyes.

I stayed very still, hardly daring to breathe. I couldn't tell if he was sincere or just working on my emotions. But I had uncovered a crack in his composure, and sensed this was my only chance to get him to talk.

Softly, I said, "It's not too late to make this right."

Talbot lifted his head, looking at me with an expression I couldn't quite read. Hope? Regret? Fear?

Before I could react, he turned and walked swiftly toward his vehicle. He started the SUV and spun out, roaring down the driveway. I stared after him, astounded. Had I gotten through to him? Or had I just let a potential murderer escape?

Chapter 33

I stood frozen for a moment, my mind racing. Had I just let Talbot slip away? Should I go after him? I discarded that thought. He'd already reached the road; his tires squealed as he made a left onto Rio Grande. I phoned Ron and gave the four-second version of what had just happened.

"Good. I'm calling Woodson right now."

I took a deep breath, steadying myself before I ran across the long front yard. Talbot might send his security detail after me at any moment. I reached my Jeep and didn't see Jenna. Then she stepped out of the bushes.

"Come on," I said, turning to her. "We gotta get out of here."

I reached into my jeans pocket for my keys and felt the lump I'd tucked into my shirt. I reached under and pulled out two thick stacks of hundred dollar bills.

"Here. From the safe. I think you've earned it."

Jenna let out a sobbing laugh, pulling me into a fierce hug. We had done it. Between the photos and the flash drive with his business records, we had found the evidence to finally put Talbot away.

We got in the Jeep and turned around to cruise past the mansion once more.

"Is there anything else you want from the house?" I asked. "We know he's not here. We can go back."

She shook her head vehemently. "Just my daughter. Once I get her back, we'll put together our own collection of mementos."

Just then, we saw law enforcement vehicles arriving. Several of them, lights flashing.

A familiar face was in the first one, his pale brown hair looking disheveled. Alan Woodson. I sighed in relief as he came to a stop and leaned out the window.

"Alan! Thank God you're here," I said. "We found what you need. There's a lot to search, between his study and the wine cellar."

Alan grinned. "No worries. I brought company." He gestured behind him as two federal agents pulled up in the next vehicle. "We have a warrant to search the entire premises."

The agents drove forward, faces set with determination. I felt a surge of relief; help was here. There would be no escape for Talbot now. We pulled into the driveway, behind all the law enforcement cars. When we stopped at the front door, I introduced Jenna, and she explained to the agents where the secrets were kept, giving combinations, passwords, and the location of the room behind the wine cellar.

"Talbot will know they've been here, and he's going to suspect me," Jenna said, as we walked back to the Jeep a few minutes later.

"He'll know I instigated this," I assured her. "I saw it in his eyes just a while ago. He's already running scared."

"Still, I'd like to stay out of sight until I know they have him. Maybe it's habit, but I don't feel safe yet."

My feeling of triumph quickly faded as I considered what was coming next. Talbot had proven himself dangerous and ruthless. Just because we had found evidence against him didn't mean he would go down without a fight.

As Jenna and I made our way out of his neighborhood, I felt a creeping unease. I kept glancing around, half expecting Talbot himself to roar out at us from a side street. Beside me, Jenna was pale and tense.

"You okay?" I asked

Jenna nodded tightly. "Let's just get out of here."

But even as we drove farther away, my earlier nonchalance evaporated. Talbot had eyes and ears everywhere. He would know what we had done.

I thought about the computer drive, which I'd handed over to Woodson. Hopefully, that small piece of evidence, along with what the agents would find inside the house, would be enough to bring Talbot to justice. Or had we just signed Jenna's death warrant by daring to cross him? I remembered his car speeding away into the night, and I couldn't let myself feel completely certain about the outcome.

Jenna looked at me as we arrived at the café where she'd left her car. "Charlie, I really hope we made the right move in trying to take Talbot down. What if I've underestimated just how far he'll go to protect himself and his secrets."

I pulled into the parking lot at the Flying Star. Despite the lateness of the hour, the place was still busy with plenty of people moving about.

Jenna sat rigidly beside me, and I knew we were both thinking the same thing—had we gotten away clean? Or was Talbot making calls, his net tightening around us already?

When he'd first come to us as a client, I hadn't noticed the cold calculation in his eyes, something that was so clear to me now. This was a man used to being in control. A man who did not tolerate defiance.

I suppressed a shiver. Don't borrow trouble, I told myself firmly. One thing at a time.

For now, we had accomplished what we came to do. We had the evidence against Talbot, and law enforcement had taken over.

By tomorrow, Jenna would go to the bank and retrieve the rest of the documents from her safe deposit box. Tonight, I would try to relax.

I looked over at Jenna and put on a smile. "So, where are you going now? Back to your friend's place?"

She nodded, still looking a little bleak.

"Would you like me to follow, just make sure you get there okay?"

"Do you mind?"

I thought of all she had risked. I could at least do this for her. "It's no problem at all. I will be right behind you."

She gave me the address, in case we should become separated at a traffic light or something, but the drive went smoothly and I watched her pull into the driveway of the little gray bungalow in the far northeast heights. Jenna hopped out of her car the moment it came to a stop in the driveway, and she leaned in my window.

"I called Adrienne on the way over. She'd love to meet you. Can you come in, maybe just for one glass of wine?"

I could see how much she'd relaxed since we parted, only twenty minutes ago. "Sure. I'd like that."

Inside, the small house felt well organized and cozy. Adrienne greeted me with a hint of reserve as she offered beverages. When Jenna excused herself to use the bathroom, her friend gave me a steady gaze.

"Please don't let my friend get hurt," she said.

It felt like a warning.

"I'm sure you have good intentions," she continued. "You seem like the type who would. But Jenna's been through so much. To an outsider, her life with Talbot looked magical. But he's not what he seems to the rest of the world."

I gave her what I hoped was a reassuring smile. "I'm quickly learning that."

"She endured a lot of verbal and emotional abuse with that man, and she never complained. But the pain went deep, soul deep. Don't let her fall into his clutches again. Please. Just help her get Kiley back. That's what she needs. And I'm sure it's what Kiley needs too."

I thought of the sullen teen I'd first met. It might take some time, but I agreed that Kiley needed her mother's influence at this point in her life.

"I will. I'll do my utmost to get Jenna back with her daughter."

Adrienne relaxed and handed me a wine glass. "Thanks."

Now I hoped I could figure out how to keep that promise.

Chapter 34

My phone was ringing when I stepped out of the shower the next morning. I pulled on a robe and saw I'd missed a call from Ron. When I called him back, he sounded excited.

"They caught Talbot trying to leave the country late last night," he said. "Woodson and two federal agents have him downtown for questioning, and Alan asked if we'd like to listen in. He thinks we might be able to fill in a few gaps or suggest questions, based on what you've learned from Jenna."

He told me where they were and I said I could be there in twenty minutes. It was a scramble to throw on some clothes, grab a granola bar, and hop in my Jeep. But the drive wasn't far and I lucked into a parking space. I spotted Ron outside an unmarked door on the third floor of the

Federal Building.

"What's happened? The last time I saw Talbot was at his house, and he raced away when I confronted him."

"You *what*?"

"I'll fill you in. Alan and the feds showed up to search the house."

Ron gave me one of his looks, the kind that said I had some 'splaining to do, but Alan came out of a nearby room at that moment.

"Good. Glad you're here," he said. "We've got Talbot in an interrogation room, and I'll put you guys in the monitoring room next to it."

"How did Talbot get from last night's little encounter to here?" I asked.

"Interesting thing," Alan said, opening the door to the room where he wanted us. "Of course, we don't know all of it yet. Sometime around midnight, he showed up at the airport, trying to catch one of the final flights of the night. TSA thought he was acting suspiciously—sweating, shaky, fumbling his documents—but his story was plausible enough and the agent passed him through. Then they checked the watch list and called us. He was sitting in the gate area for a flight to Toronto when we caught up."

"Toronto?" Ron asked.

"Claimed it was a quick trip for a client meeting. Like, what car dealer has 'client meetings' in other countries?" Alan pointed to a large window in the wall, where we could see Talbot seated at a basic gray metal table. "I'll let you listen in," he said, flipping a switch for the audio.

Two men in suits stood on either side of Talbot, badges on their belts.

"You know why you're here, Mr. Farber," said the older agent gruffly. He had a no-nonsense look about him.

Talbot sat, gripping the arms of the metal chair. "I don't. What is this about?" he asked.

The agent ignored his question. "Federal authorities got a warrant to search your residence. Officers went there last night."

Talbot tugged at his tie, visibly losing some of his cool composure.

"I don't know what you think you'll find," he said, trying to sound casual.

The agent leaned forward, his eyes boring into Talbot. "Oh, I think they found plenty. The guns, for starters."

Talbot's jaw worked back and forth, and he reached for the glass of water on the table.

I smiled. "Looking a little rattled, isn't he? He thinks he's been so careful."

"Guns? I don't know what you mean," Talbot said.

The agent smirked. "Of course not. The AR-15s stashed in that secret room won't be any surprise then."

Talbot swallowed hard at the mention of the hidden room behind the wine cellar.

"It doesn't look good that you were trying to leave the country, either," said the second agent.

"That was business. I told that to airport security. Already, I'm missing a very important meeting in Toronto. Once I get hold of your superiors, you'll have some answering to do."

"Is that right?" The older agent placed a hand on his hip. "Then I guess you'll just have to report me. Meanwhile, we have your passport and you're not getting it back anytime soon. You can decide if you want to use your one phone call to explain to your client."

Talbot crossed his arms and stared back silently.

Chapter 35

Jenna listened as her call went to voicemail. "Hey, it's Kiley. You know what to do. Or just text me!"

She'd tried that. Several texts and three previous calls. Nothing drew a response. She knew Charlie had talked to Kiley, paving the way for what she hoped would be a positive mother-daughter reunion.

"I guess I just have to face it. She doesn't want to talk to me." Jenna turned to Adrienne with tears in her eyes. She'd been caressing the pale blue sweater ever since she returned from Talbot's place last night.

Her friend came around the end of the kitchen counter and placed an arm around Jenna's shoulder. "Sweetie, it could be anything. Her battery died and she's lost her charger. It's gotta be something like that."

Her phone rang, startling both of them.

"It's Charlie," Jenna whispered, accepting the call. "What's up?"

"The feds have Talbot. Ron and I are listening in on the questioning. So far, he's tried to explain away his movements, and so far, they haven't actually arrested him. I just wanted you to know."

"Thanks. Look, you haven't heard from Kiley today, have you?"

"No, but I wouldn't expect to. You've tried calling her?"

"Several times." Jenna took a deep breath. "I know. Could be any number of reasons."

"Are you comfortable calling the Farbers? She's staying at their house. Maybe they still have a landline?"

"Let me think about that. I always got along well with Talbot's parents, but after all that's happened, I don't know what their attitude will be."

"Okay, gotta go. It looks like the lead investigator is walking back into the room." Charlie hung up and Jenna turned back to Adrienne.

"What do you think? Should I try talking to the grandparents?"

"Is there any harm in it? I mean, what's the worst that can happen? They tell you to buzz off and then hang up? They refuse to let you talk to Kiley?" Adrienne shrugged. "Or maybe they're happy for Kiley's sake that her mother is alive and well. And maybe they'll even agree to meet somewhere with you."

"I'll never know unless I try. That's what you're saying."

"That's exactly what I'm saying." Adrienne picked up her purse. "I've got a few errands to run. I wish you luck."

Jenna picked up her phone and closed her eyes, pulling up a memory of the long-forgotten phone number. She tapped in the number and waited.

Chapter 36

Ron and I stood once again by the mirrored window. The show was getting interesting.

"Why hasn't he called his lawyer?" I whispered.

"Probably thinks he's so brilliant he can talk his way out of anything," Detective Woodson said. "The cocky ones often have that attitude."

Talbot sat up straighter. It was almost as if he'd heard Alan.

The younger agent spoke up. "Let's try this again, Mr. Farber. Why don't you tell us about the guns?" His tone was stern but not threatening.

Talbot sighed. "All right, yes. I have weapons. For protection."

The older agent raised an eyebrow. "That's quite an arsenal just for protection. Were you anticipating a small army invasion?"

Talbot shook his head. "It's not like that. I have ... enemies. Powerful ones. I need to defend myself."

"With assault rifles?" The agent sounded skeptical.

"Desperate times call for desperate measures," Talbot said quietly.

The agents exchanged a look, like, oh please. The younger one leaned forward. "Help us understand then. Who are these enemies?"

Talbot hesitated, clearly deciding how much to reveal. Enough to justify the guns, but not to incriminate himself further?

"Business rivals mostly," he began carefully. "Jealous of my success. They've made threats. I took precautions, that's all."

The agents listened, stone-faced. Everyone could see beads of sweat forming on their suspect's forehead.

Talbot fidgeted with his hands, trying to think of what to say next. The agents stared at him, waiting.

Finally, the older agent broke the silence. "Look, we've got a number of potential charges here," he said gravely.

I almost found it humorous to watch the change in his demeanor. This was really happening.

"Given the number and type of firearms found, you could be looking at felony charges of possessing assault weapons and illegal possession of firearms," the agent continued. "Computer forensics are right now looking at your computer browsing history, and we have reason to believe you have customers who are right-wing extremists dealing on the dark web."

"I have a federal firearms dealer license," Talbot informed them smugly, "and what you're threatening is not true under the law here."

One strike against the agents, who apparently thought they could bluff him.

Talbot opened his mouth to bluster his way through, but the agent held up a hand to stop him.

"I'm afraid your license has been revoked. And that's not even considering your ... other history." The agent gave Talbot a pointed look.

The color drained from Talbot's face.

"With your wife's disappearance, we could potentially charge you with attempted murder, conspiracy to commit murder, and then there's domestic terrorism ..." The agent trailed off, letting the severity of the words sink in.

I could almost feel sorry for the man. Talbot looked queasy as he contemplated the agent's words. This changed everything. His money, his connections—none of it would save him now.

I turned to Alan. "They've found all that?"

He nodded. "And more. Among the documents Jenna handed over, there are records of high-interest payments that smack of loan sharking. Plus, offshore accounts. He's been laundering money for years. For drug cartels, weapon smugglers ... dangerous people."

I sucked in a sharp breath. This changed everything. Talbot had always seemed like a respectable businessman, a pillar of the community. Learning the extent of his crimes, after we'd agreed to represent him, made me feel a little sick. I exchanged a look with Ron and then turned my attention back to the observation window.

"I'd suggest you start cooperating fully and truthfully," the agent finished. "It's your only chance for leniency at this point."

A muscle in Talbot's jaw clenched and unclenched. "I want my lawyer."

Chapter 37

Grace Farber answered on the second ring. Jenna took a deep breath.

"Grace, it's Jenna. I know I have a lot of explaining—"

"Yes, you do."

Cracking the shell around her in-laws would not be easy, if she could do it at all.

"I need to speak to Kiley, please."

"Jenna—"

"I'm her mother, and even though I may not be the best one ever, I still have the right to talk to her."

"We'll not go into the quality of your mothering," Grace said, her voice cold. "That's a conversation for another time. Kiley isn't here."

"Is she with friends? She's not answering her phone and I'm worried."

There was a long pause. "No, she isn't with friends. At least I don't think so. Didn't you know? Talbot picked her up last evening. He seemed very shaken up and said he wanted her at home. I would assume you two could at least—"

Jenna ended the call and immediately dialed Charlie's number. Her voice was shaking so hard she could barely get the words out. "He's taken Kiley."

Chapter 38

I must have uttered a curse word because both Ron and Alan Woodson were staring at me.

"What's wrong?" Ron asked, reading the look on my face.

In just a few words I told him. "How? Agents have been searching his house all night. He was at the airport first thing this morning ... So, what has he done with her?"

The fact that Kiley wasn't answering her phone was worrisome. Teens live on their phones. Even if Talbot had planned to have his daughter go with him to Canada, she would have her phone with her. And how would that work, anyway? Talbot had been pulled over at the security line and no one mentioned a teen girl traveling with him.

My thoughts all piled up and came out in a rush of questions directed at Ron, who put a hand out to steady me.

"You go to Jenna and work with her. Maybe one of you will come up with some ideas. Make sure she's in a safe place. I'll stay here and see how the drama unfolds. Once Talbot's lawyer appears, I expect there'll be some action."

"Okay, good idea. I told Jenna to stay where she is, but it wouldn't surprise me if she just takes off driving, trying to find her kid."

I rushed to the elevator and took it to the ground floor, tapping Jenna's number as I walked toward the lot where I'd parked my Jeep.

"Are you still at … your friend's house?" I asked, glancing every which way, hoping no one nearby happened to be on Talbot's legal team. I didn't, for one minute, believe he had only one lawyer on this problem.

"Yes, I am," Jenna said. "I can't think what to do next."

"Okay, we're going to work on that together. I'm on my way. Stay right where you are."

I heard a sob at the other end and hoped she would follow instruction. No one in her mental state should be driving.

Traffic was a mess on the interstate, and it took me a while to get to Adrienne's neighborhood. Somewhere along the way I realized I hadn't eaten breakfast and it was already past noon. I debated stopping for some kind of takeout food but was afraid any delay would be a reason for Jenna to leave.

She'd probably head straight for Talbot's house, in the hope that Kiley would be safe and sound there. It didn't make any sense, but Jenna's mindset at this point was just to act, not to think first. I breathed a sigh of relief when I arrived at Adrienne's house and saw two cars in the driveway. One was Jenna's little sedan.

Adrienne let me in and asked if I wanted some lunch.

She and Jenna were having a sandwich in the kitchen. I thanked her and headed in that direction.

Jenna's sandwich was untouched. She had a potato chip halfway to her mouth when I walked into the room, but she dropped that back to her plate.

Adrienne quickly assembled another sandwich and handed me the plate. We took seats at the table with Jenna.

"Please eat," our hostess pleaded. "You can't make decisions or go running around in all directions on an empty stomach."

We both smiled at her persistence, and I had to agree. The thin-sliced ham was so tasty that once I started eating it, I couldn't quit. Between mouthfuls, I explained that I'd been at the federal building where they were questioning Talbot about all the evidence that had been gathered at his home.

"When I left, he'd called for his attorney. Ron's waiting to see how that goes."

"Is he under arrest?" Jenna asked.

"Not yet. At this point they're just questioning him. It was when the talk turned to filing specific charges that he shut up and wanted the lawyer." I smiled a little at the memory. "Up to that point, he was pretty confident he could talk his way out of everything."

"But the big question—where is Kiley?" Jenna said she had already called the grandparents, which was how she found out Talbot had picked up their daughter.

"He was at the airport, ready to take a flight to Toronto, when the agents detained him," I said. "If Kiley was with him, she got away. But he didn't say anything about her during the whole interrogation. He must have taken her somewhere else. Who are her closest friends?"

I knew, the moment I said it, that was the wrong question for Jenna. She burst into tears. "I don't even know. I don't even know who my own daughter's friends are …"

Adrienne reached over and put an arm around her shoulders, pulling Jenna close.

"Let me try with the grandparents," I said. I picked up Jenna's phone and memorized the number she had last dialed.

Calling from my own phone, at least Grace Farber picked up the call.

"Grace, it's Charlie Parker. We met yesterday when you picked up Kiley."

Her voice was a little frosty at first, but when I explained the necessity of finding Kiley—leaving out the part about Talbot being quizzed by federal agents—she readily shared names of two of her granddaughter's friends. When I pressed a little harder, I also got their numbers.

But the moment's elation was quickly squashed when I called each of the friends. Neither had heard from Kiley since the previous day. One girl, Hannah, had spoken to her when she was on her way to her grandparents' home.

That was the last either of them had heard from her.

Chapter 39

Two attorneys walked in, three-piece suits, pinstripes, briefcases, and all. Ron turned to Alan Woodson. "Is this now privileged conversation?"

"Not until they make the agents leave. Let's just see how it plays out."

The two lawyers sat down, one on each side of their client. The older agent resumed the questioning.

"Back to the cache of weapons that were found in your home," he said.

Talbot spread his hands. "You have to listen to me," he implored the agent. "This is all a huge misunderstanding. Those weapons weren't mine. I was just ... holding them for a friend."

The agent regarded him skeptically. "That's not what you told us earlier. A friend? What's this friend's name?"

Talbot faltered. "I, uh, can't say. Client confidentiality."

The agent shook his head. "That's not going to cut it, Mr. Farber. You need to give me something—anything—that can corroborate your story."

Talbot glanced at each of the attorneys, but they let him go on. What could he say? What could possibly get him out of this mess?

"The ... the ammunition!" he blurted out. "None of it matches those guns you found. I don't even own any ammo."

Ron and Alan exchanged a look. What a story. It was a long shot, but it was apparently all Talbot had.

The agent considered this for a moment. "We'll see about that," he finally said. He motioned to one of the officers. "Bag all the ammunition separately. We'll need to analyze it back at the lab."

Talbot seemed to suppress a sigh of relief. The lawyers conferred behind their hands.

Ron's phone rang. Charlie. "What's up?"

"No one knows where Kiley is. I've checked with the grandparents and with her closest friends. Can you ask the agents to pin Talbot down? What's his story after he picked her up last night? If he can't come up with something good, we should consider pressing for an Amber Alert for her."

"Got it," Ron said. He turned to Alan and repeated the whole conversation.

Woodson hurried out of the viewing room and tapped on the door to the room where the agents were. The younger one stepped out and they conferred in the hallway for a moment. When he returned, he turned on Talbot.

"Where is your daughter?" he demanded, none too friendly about it. He glanced up at the lawyers and told them what had transpired.

Talbot barely blinked an eye. "She is completely safe."

"Where?"

"In my care."

"You, sir, are about to be arrested, if you keep this up. I ask again, where is your daughter?"

Talbot leaned toward the more senior of the lawyers and they whispered for a few seconds. Then the lawyer spoke up.

"My client has answered your question. And now, unless you are prepared to arrest him on specific charges, not this silly game of fishing for non-existent evidence of non-existent crimes, we're done here."

Both attorneys stood, and Talbot followed suit. The agents seemed resigned to the fact that he was about to walk out.

Ron stepped out into the hall, where Alan intercepted him. "He can't go far. We've confiscated his passport, and he'll be under surveillance. He'd be a fool to leave the city now."

Chapter 40

The ringing of Adrienne's doorbell made us all jump. Jenna's face went white, her eyes wide like a trapped animal.

"It's just Ron. I told him where we were," I said, but my voice shook a little. Jenna had barely eaten any lunch. We were all on edge, hoping Talbot would be locked up, and not knowing where Kiley was.

Adrienne answered the door and Ron's footsteps followed her into the living room. He appeared in the doorway, his expression grim. "Talbot's attorneys played hardball. He's out."

Jenna squeezed her eyes shut, a tear slipping down her cheek. She wrapped her arms around herself and rocked back and forth, as if trying to self-soothe.

I moved to sit beside her on the sofa, rubbing her back

gently. "Hey, it's okay. You're safe here."

She shook her head, eyes still closed. "No. He's using Kiley as bait to get me out in the open. Next time, he really will succeed in killing me."

Ron dragged a hand over his face. "Jenna's right. Money like his buys influence. He won't stop until he finds her."

Jenna let out a choked sob, burying her face in her hands.

I shot my brother a look and pulled her into a hug. "Shh. We won't let him get to you," I murmured. But my confidence was just a front. Talbot had connections everywhere. How long could we really hide her?

Jenna lifted her head, eyes red-rimmed but determined. "I won't go back there. Never again." Her voice hardened. "He doesn't own me. Not anymore."

Jenna's hands curled into fists, knuckles white, as anger took over. "All these years he's been lying to Kiley about me. Telling her I just up and abandoned her." She shook her head, fresh tears welling. "My little girl probably hates me."

I chose my next words carefully. "Kiley is smarter than Talbot gives her credit for. Deep down, she knows something isn't right."

Jenna wiped her eyes, sniffling. "I hope so. I just …" Her voice broke. "I missed so much. Her first day of school, her first date. All of it."

She took a shaky breath, and when she spoke again, her tone was icy. "Well not anymore. I'm taking my life back. And, now that we know the extent of his illegal activities, I'll have the proof I need to get my daughter away from that monster."

"The authorities are working on it, Jenna," I assured her.

"But it will take them a long time to build a case and take him to court," she protested. "In the meantime, I have to find my baby."

"Just don't do anything rash," I cautioned. "The police are aware she's missing. They're putting out an alert."

Ron nodded. "We've got your back, Jenna. Talbot has money, but we've got resources too. We'll figure this out."

A tiny smile touched Jenna's lips. The fear was still there in her eyes, but now a spark of determination shone through.

Ron headed for the door. "I've got things to do at the office, so I'll leave you ladies here. I'll report any news that comes through about Kiley."

Adrienne also got up. "I promised a client I'd meet with them at the furniture gallery. They're almost at the end of a big reno job and choosing the furniture is the final step. I really can't cancel on them again."

"Don't worry," Jenna told her. She gave me the same look. "Really. I lived on my own in the back woods of Alaska for a lot of years. I can entertain myself for one afternoon in a house with cable TV, for gosh sake."

I felt uneasy about leaving her, warning her again not to go out looking for Kiley on her own. "Even if—*especially* if—she turns up back at Talbot's house, you do not want to be in the middle of that. Talbot is probably furious about getting caught and questioned. Stay out of his way. I'm serious."

"Yes, ma'am," she said, smiling. "I'm going to let the police do their job. Those agents, the ones you described questioning him, they'll put together a strong case. I'm sure of it."

I looked sideways at her. "You're not just saying that to get me out of here, are you?"

Her face relaxed. "No. I'm really not. It's mostly that I'm a little socialized-out. I haven't spent this many days with this many people in years. I could use some time on my own, just to think and decompress." A tiny smile crossed her face. "If Adrienne had a woodchopping block out back, I'd be making use of it."

"Okay. I can totally understand that." And I did. There were many times, especially when a case dragged out and there was travel involved, that I longed for a few hours of peace and quiet. "I'm going. You have my number in your contacts. You *will* call me if anything unexpected comes up."

Together, we checked all the windows and doors so I could assure myself she was tucked in, safe and snug. Then I went out to my Jeep and took the long route home. An afternoon of peace and quiet held a lot of appeal for me right now, too.

At home, I wrestled with Freckles and then took her for a short walk. A cup of tea and a mushy movie on *Lifetime* were the perfect antidote, and I was well into full relaxation mode when my phone rang.

"Charlie, it's Adrienne. Please tell me Jenna's with you."

"Um, no." A shiver went through me as I sat up, on full alert.

"Please tell me you gave her a ride somewhere and you know exactly where she is."

"Adrienne, what's happened?"

"Ohmygod, ohmygod."

"Calm down a minute and just tell me what you see."

"I just got home. Her car is in the driveway. The living room is a mess. Not a sloppy-person mess. The coffee table's broken, papers and pillows are all scattered. It looks like the back door was kicked in."

Oh crap. I knew I shouldn't have left her.

"Call the police," I told her. "Wait there and tell them we felt Jenna was in danger. I'll be there as fast as I can."

Chapter 41

Three cop cars sat in front of Adrienne's house when I got there. Extra points for a quick response time, I thought. There sat Jenna's little sedan in the driveway. One of the officers was standing near it, writing something in her little notebook.

Alan Woodson stood in the front hall.

"They have Major Crimes responding to missing persons reports now?" I asked, with a friendly nudge.

"When the subject's name is Farber, yes."

The female officer came in from the driveway. "Any chance the missing woman just left with a friend, maybe a quick run to the grocery store?"

All of us gave her a steady stare.

"Okay," she backtracked, "it doesn't look that way."

"But it's a good point," I said, turning to Adrienne.

"Have you tried calling her cell phone?"

She nodded bleakly. "It was the first thing I did. When it rang, I found it under the sofa. And her purse is in the guest room where she's staying."

Despite her panic, Adrienne had acted logically and checked things before calling for help. I reached out and squeezed her hand.

"This has to be Talbot's doing," I said to Woodson. "She's been terrified of him."

"We just released him a few hours ago," Alan said, "Would he really take the chance of coming directly here—if he even knew where to find her?"

"His men, then. He'd send someone."

Alan turned to the lead officer in the house. "Get a couple squad cars out to the Talbot home on Rio Grande and have them check the place for any signs of Mrs. Farber."

"I just don't understand how he would have known she was staying here." Adrienne was wringing the life out of a tissue she'd been holding ever since I arrived. "We were so careful."

I nodded, facing Alan. "She's right. Jenna was super cautious from the moment I located her in Alaska. She had identification under a different name and everything."

The officers seemed to be finished taking fingerprints and photos of the scene. They'd even found a boot print on the back door, near the deadbolt lock, where someone with some strength had shattered the doorframe.

"I guess we're done here," Alan said, as the others exited. "I'll let you know of any developments."

That didn't exactly reassure me.

I turned to Adrienne as we watched the cruisers drive away. "Do you want to come home with me?"

She shook her head. "I've got a locksmith on the way to fix the back door. He's a handyman I've used with a lot of my design projects. He'll bring lumber and a new lock."

"I can stay with you, if you'd like."

"It's fine, Charlie. Talbot or his guys, they got what they came for. I don't feel like I'm in danger."

"Oh, Adrienne, I feel so badly that you got pulled into this."

She stepped back from my hug and gripped my shoulders. "Jenna has been my friend for a very long time. I knew things weren't good for her, ever since before Kiley was born. I'd do anything for her."

"I know. Thank you for being there."

"You go on home. You've had a pretty eventful week or two yourself. Once my buddy has the back door repaired, I'm going to set the alarm and close myself in here with my mom's enchiladas from the freezer and an evening of movies."

"You're sure?"

"Positive."

A truck pulled up in front of the house just then. *Jake The Handyman* was painted on its side, and the guy who got out greeted Adrienne familiarly. I said goodbye and headed back toward my end of town.

I was approaching the exit for my neighborhood, where I would normally make a left, when it hit me that if I turned right and went somewhat—okay, a few miles— out of my way, I could scope out the Farber house. Just checking, you know. See if the police were there. See if any action was happening. Drake would probably lecture me for this, but he doesn't necessarily need to know.

The late afternoon traffic was a little heavier than I'd expected, but within twenty minutes I was approaching the entry to the huge property. I cruised by as slowly as I could, incurring a couple of angry horn blasts, but I didn't see any action at the mansion.

No cop cars, no Talbot vehicles, nothing.

I swung to the side of the road and waited for a chance to double back. When I got the break in the traffic I needed, I passed the place again, this time traveling southerly. Two APD cruisers were just now making the turn into the long driveway.

Okay, better late than never. I found a wide spot in the road and pulled aside to watch. I could see the cops making their way toward the house, then they were blocked from view by the trees and shrubs. A big part of me wanted to follow them, to be right there and see what happened next. But common sense won out. Getting into the middle of a potential shootout would not be smart.

Ten minutes passed. I pictured the officers approaching the door and knocking. Waiting for a response. Maybe Talbot would answer, and most likely he would come up with a plausibly innocent-sounding alibi. The house was huge and there was at least one secret room, that I knew of. Without a warrant and a big SWAT team, the odds were Jenna could be right there and no one would figure it out.

Worse—as my mind went into overdrive—I pictured Talbot ordering a couple of his thugs to nab Jenna from Adrienna's house, take her out into the desert somewhere and leave her body to be discovered by the buzzards. I squeezed my eyes shut and forced that vision away. When I opened them again, I saw the two cruisers leaving the Talbot property.

No lights, sirens, or whoopla. From their profile view, none of the officers seemed agitated. It was as if they'd just checked one more item off their to-do list and were now getting on with their evening. When I got home, I'd call Alan Woodson and see what the police had reported.

Just for reassurance, I phoned Adrienne to check in. She hadn't heard a word from Jenna and was worried about her. Otherwise, all was well enough. At home, Drake had seasoned a couple of steaks and was ready to put them on the grill as soon as I arrived. I told him what had happened with Talbot and Jenna, but there were so many details to this very long day it was too much to cover in depth. I switched the topic to his work and we had a peaceful meal.

My after-dinner call to Alan didn't net much that I hadn't already figured out. The officers reported that Mr. Farber did not appear to be at home. They had knocked at both front and back doors, had seen no lights, no vehicles, or other signs of life. I felt a bit skeptical about that. Talbot could have easily seen them coming and just laid low, waiting for them to leave. He'd been questioned all morning and certainly wouldn't invite more. But I didn't voice all my thoughts. What was the point?

Eventually, I went to bed, trying to stop my thoughts from churning. Somewhere around three a.m. I fell into a restless sleep.

* * *

In the dream I was chasing Jenna around the side of that motel we'd stayed at in Anchorage. I was catching up with her when she spun around and shouted at me: "Get away. I don't want to be found! You'll tell him!"

Her anger was so vivid, I stopped in my tracks. And that's when I woke up. My bedside clock said it was 4:17 a.m.

You'll tell him. The dream words echoed in my head.

Had I? I sat up so suddenly that Drake moaned in his sleep beside me. I got out of bed and went into the bathroom, turning on only a night light. Had I somehow been the one who told Talbot how to find Jenna yesterday?

When I spoke with Ron on the phone, giving him Adrienne's address, had Talbot somehow overheard? Ron was still at the federal building when we spoke; he often puts his phone on speaker—maybe he had. I hadn't thought to ask; I just blabbed away with the address. Oh God. I felt sick.

With my head pounding, I pulled on my fuzzy robe and tiptoed through the bedroom, trying hard not to wake Freckles or Drake. The dog raised her head and plopped back down again. Drake snored and rolled over. In the kitchen, I stared out the window, my stomach in knots. Ever since Adrienne's phone call yesterday, I'd been second-guessing myself.

A lack of sleep and my roiling thoughts weren't helping. I wrapped my arms around myself, wishing I could take back my words. Jenna had begged me to keep her location a secret. She'd fled that cruise ship thirteen years ago for a reason. Who was I to drag her back to the life she'd fought so hard to escape?

I brewed a single cup of coffee, but it tasted like acid and after a few sips I dumped it down the drain. I'm not normally a person who anguishes a lot, more of a doer than a regretter. But I was momentarily at a loss. If the police couldn't find Jenna, how would I?

"Morning," Drake mumbled as he shuffled into the kitchen. Light was just beginning to show in the eastern sky, outlining the crest of Sandia Peak. He paused, blinking the sleep from his eyes. "You okay? You look like you've seen a ghost."

I forced a tight smile. "I'm fine. Just didn't sleep well."

Drake studied my face. He could always see right through me. I braced for the questions, but he simply kissed my cheek and squeezed my shoulder.

"Want me to make you some tea?"

I nodded, thankful for his tact. If I was going to share my thoughts with anyone, it would be him. But I felt like I had to figure this out on my own first. I turned the conversation around to ask about his plans for the day.

There was something about a meeting with someone at the Forest Service. The fire season would start soon, and he wanted to get his bid in for any work that came along. I heard a fraction of it, hoping that I nodded at all the right times.

After swallowing down a slice of toast with my tea, I left Drake standing in the kitchen and went to get dressed, each mundane task requiring immense effort. Brush teeth. Comb hair. Get dressed. Just keep moving. Breathe.

But the doubts followed me, whispering that I'd ruined Jenna's life all over again.

* * *

I sat at my desk, staring blankly at the computer screen. The cursor blinked accusingly. You did this. This is your fault.

"Morning, Charlie!"

I flinched as Ron breezed into my office, two coffees in hand. "Brought you a latte. Figured you could use a pick-me-up after last night."

I forced a smile and took the coffee. "Thanks."

"Is there any news about Jenna or Kiley?"

I shook my head and felt my eyes prickle a little.

Ron pressed. "Charlie, share with me. Let's talk about it."

I told him about my early morning realization, that I might have been the one to give away Jenna's safe hiding place.

He shook his head. "I didn't have my phone on speaker. That wasn't it." Then his face paled. "Oh crap. I might have said it out loud. I pulled out my notebook to write it down. Do you remember me repeating the address back to you? I think I might have."

I nodded. He was right. "I should have asked if you were alone when we spoke."

"I thought I was, pretty much. I was standing in the lobby after leaving the interrogation rooms. Talbot and his lawyers had walked out ahead of me. They'd left through the front door."

And probably some of Talbot's men had been right behind. "We can't change that. It's done. I'm just trying to figure out what to do next."

My phone buzzed with a new text.

Adrienne: Any word about Jenna? Call me.

I groaned inwardly. Adrienne must have been through a bad night, at least as bad as mine. I called and she picked up immediately. We exchanged how-are-you and each gave tepid responses.

"I feel so badly that we involved you in this," I told her. "Ron and I took this case. We should have solved it."

"Jenna involved me, and she did so because we're close. She's the nearest to a sister that I have, and I'd do anything for her. I don't want to be shut out."

"I didn't mean it that way. I'll keep you in the loop if we learn anything new." It probably went without saying, but I added, "And please let me know the very minute you hear anything."

I hung up, feeling a sort of renewed energy. I wasn't the same woman who stumbled blindly into this mess weeks ago. Talbot had lied, had underestimated me, dismissing me as someone with a far inferior intellect to his. But I was getting closer to the truth now. And I was ready to fight him. My circle of support was small, but growing.

I swigged the last of the coffee Ron had brought me. Across the hall, I could hear voices, a phone call. I walked over to his office to see what was going on. He ended the call and turned to me.

"That was Woodson. I called him to see if there was an update."

I felt my heart race a little.

"Nothing on Jenna or Kiley yet. But his computer experts have been evaluating that hard drive you and Jenna turned over. The files decrypted easily enough. They've got bank statements, wire transfers, emails. Not enough to turn over to the prosecutor yet, but a trail seems to be emerging."

"And Talbot? Are they watching him?"

"I don't know details. It sounds like they at least know that he returned home last night, probably after a late dinner somewhere."

So he hadn't been hiding out in the house when the police showed up, late in the afternoon. Well, maybe. I decided to keep all the options open until I could prove something.

My phone rang, pulling me back to my office. Hm. It was an unfamiliar number.

Chapter 42

"Charlie? It's Grace Farber. Don't hang up—I want to help you."

I sat in my chair to steady myself. Why was Talbot's mother calling me? But if she really wanted to help ... this could be the breakthrough I needed.

"I'm listening," I said. "What made you change your mind?" I asked Grace bluntly. "You've stood by Talbot this whole time."

Grace sighed heavily. "Because the lies have gone on long enough. What he did to Jenna ... what he's still doing ... it's not right."

I had a sudden vision, of Grace sitting in an elegant living room with Talbot standing there and directing the conversation.

"Can I meet you somewhere?"

A pause. "Well … I'm out doing errands. I'm nearly finished at Walgreens, then I'm going to the carwash."

"Carwash is good. Which one?"

"San Mateo and Central."

"I'll be there in fifteen minutes." It would give us a good noisy place to converse without appearing to. A place that would appear to be an entirely random meeting, should anyone happen to see us.

I pulled into the parking lot of a strip shopping center next door, parked to face the carwash entrance, and waited for Grace Farber. About a minute later, she pulled in and got into the line. I followed suit. My Jeep would go through the automated wash within one or two cars after hers. I told the attendant I wanted the most basic wash, then walked into the building.

There stood Grace. My pulse quickened as I casually walked over and stood beside her at the windows where customers watch their cars go through the process. "Tell me what you know."

She faced forward, not looking at me. "Talbot knows the investigation has turned. He's having you followed, Charlie. You and your partner."

I swore under my breath. I should have expected this.

"There's more." Grace's voice dropped. "I overheard him talking about a safehouse."

"What safehouse? Where?"

"I don't know. He owns a number of properties, some residential rentals, some commercial. But something he said made me think he's got Kiley at one he owns in Placitas."

How far did this man's reach extend? "Keep your voice low. I'm going to ask you for directions to the nearest mall, but I need you to respond with the address of this place where you think she is."

Another customer came in, a large man in casual clothing. Grace moved farther along in the wait line. I followed, leaving the man near the cashier's stand to pay for his wash. The moment I caught up with Grace, she whispered an address. Inside the noisy carwash, I hoped I heard it right.

"I don't know any details. But Charlie ... be careful. Talbot didn't get where he is by playing nice."

My mind raced with the implications. The safehouse could be the breakthrough I needed to find Kiley. I couldn't assume she was actually safe there, even if it was her own father who took her there. Talbot was clearly rattled if he had sicced his security team on me. I could practically hear the clock ticking.

I thanked Grace tersely and walked out to claim my Jeep. Now I needed to lose the tail, and I was going to check out that safehouse tonight.

Chapter 43

I waited until normal closing time at the office before leaving. I'd made some calls and arranged to borrow vehicles. By now, my Jeep would certainly be recognizable by Talbot's men. By six o'clock I drove through the gathering dusk in a tan sedan that belonged to a neighbor, my knuckles white on the steering wheel.

The little town of Placitas was twenty minutes north of Albuquerque, and the address Grace had given was down an unmarked dirt road that wound through rocky hills studded with juniper trees. I'd changed cars and outerwear twice, using every evasive driving technique I knew, and I hadn't spotted a tail.

Finally, I killed the headlights and crept up the long driveway, parking behind a copse of piñon trees. The house was dark. No sign of guards that I could see. I slipped on gloves and grabbed my lockpick set and small flashlight. Getting inside was easy—too easy. The alarm system wasn't even armed. Within minutes I was moving silently through the dark rooms, my Beretta aimed forward, searching for any clue to confirm this was Kiley's prison.

In one bedroom I spotted blonde hairs on a pillow. Makeup and clothes that matched her size. I felt around and found a journal under the mattress. I set the Beretta down and opened the book. It was filled with Kiley's looping handwriting.

Kiley had definitely been here. But where was she now?

I flipped through the journal rapidly. The most recent entries were deeply unsettling. Kiley wrote of being a prisoner, never allowed to leave or make contact with anyone. And Talbot's threats against Jenna if she tried to escape.

So, Kiley and Jenna had not made contact. I surmised that he must be holding Jenna somewhere else.

Rage boiled up in me. That monster. Holding his own wife and child hostage through fear and intimidation. But now I had the evidence I needed. If I could only find both women, hopefully safe and sound.

I pulled out my phone to snap a few pictures. I could call Alan Woodson and have this place processed as a crime scene. As I did, a noise at the window made me whirl. A dark figure stood there, shockingly familiar.

I grabbed my pistol and shined my flashlight at the face. It was definitely Kiley, though she looked thinner and more haggard than when I'd last seen her. Her eyes went wide with fear as she took in the gun aimed at her.

"Kiley, it's me, Charlie," I said in a fierce whisper, lowering my weapon. "You're safe now."

She sagged against the window frame in relief. "Oh,

thank God. I saw someone break in and I thought …" She shuddered. "How did you find me?"

"It's a long story. But we need to get you out of here." I grabbed her hand and led her swiftly down the hall. She followed without resistance, stumbling a little in her weakness.

We were almost to the back door when a blinding light switched on, illuminating the mudroom. I shoved Kiley behind me and aimed my gun toward the light. A familiar smooth voice spoke.

"Well, well. What do we have here?"

Talbot. He stood silhouetted in the doorway, two hulking men flanking him. Not one silver hair was out of place. My heart pounded, but I kept my gun steady.

"It's over, Talbot," I said. "We have everything needed to expose what you've done."

He chuckled softly. "Oh, I don't think so. In fact, I'd say you've made a tragic mistake coming here tonight. A mistake that will cost you dearly."

His gaze focused somewhere behind me and he nodded. Before I could react, a cloth covered my nose and mouth. Chloroform. I struggled wildly, but it was no use. Somewhere in the distance, I heard Kiley shriek. The drug overwhelmed my senses and the world went black.

Chapter 44

I blinked slowly, trying to clear the fog from my brain. My head throbbed and my mouth felt like cotton. As my eyes focused, I realized I was tied to a chair in a dimly lit room.

Jenna was next to me, similarly bound, unconscious. No sign of Kiley. I strained against the ropes but they held fast. How could I have been so careless? I should have known Talbot would be guarding Kiley and watching for me.

The door creaked open and Talbot strolled in, an amused smile on his face.

"Awake at last, I see. You've caused quite a bit of trouble for me, Charlie. I'd love to know how you acquired such ... damaging information."

Little did he know. I glared at him. "Your secrets aren't

as well-hidden as you think. But you won't get away with this. Too many people know."

He laughed. "You think so? We're miles from anywhere, my dear. No one knows you're here. Or cares."

Cold fear trickled down my spine, but I forced myself to stay calm. "You're wrong. I made arrangements, just in case. If I don't check in soon, there's even more evidence. Everything will go public."

A flicker of doubt crossed his face before the smug smile returned. "A bluff. You have nothing."

"What about the police, and the feds? Do you really think that interrogation session yesterday was just for fun?"

"Basically. Nothing they have will stick. I have the best lawyers in the Southwest. And your supposed evidence … come on. What could you have that goes beyond what those downtown bozos have?"

I raised my chin. "Try me."

For a long moment, he studied me. Then he turned on his heel.

"No matter. You won't be checking in with anyone, ever again."

He left, slamming the heavy door behind him. I sagged against the ropes, mind racing. I had to get us out of here.

A soft groan made me twist toward Jenna. Her eyelids fluttered open and she looked around in confusion.

"Where are we?" she croaked.

"Talbot's got us." I looked around but didn't recognize this as a room in the mansion or the house where I'd found Kiley. "Have you been in this same spot all along? Did he bring you here directly from Adrienne's house?"

At the mention of her friend, Jenna sagged. "Two men … huge brutes I didn't know. Happened so fast …

chased me down, and put something over my face."

"Was it sickly sweet smelling?" The same chloroform they'd used on me. "Don't tell me he's kept you sitting in that chair, drugged, the whole time?"

She appeared confused. "… think so. Not sure."

"Jenna, take some deep breaths. Get some air and try to clear your head. We're going to have to work together to get out of here."

Jenna's eyes widened in fear but she nodded silently and followed my directions. We would find a way out of this. We had to.

I resumed struggling against the ropes, straining until my wrists were raw. But it was no use. Clearly, I wasn't going anywhere until I could get free. I scanned the room, searching for anything sharp. It seemed like a storeroom of some kind, except there wasn't much in it other than the two chairs we were tied to. Concrete walls and floor, cold and damp feeling, with a long fluorescent light fixture overhead. At least Talbot had not turned it off when he walked out.

My eyes landed on an old pipe running along the wall, jagged and rusted. If I could just reach it …

I scooted the chair, inch by inch, across the floor, grunting with effort. The pipe seemed impossibly far but I kept scooting. I had to try.

At last, my fingers brushed the cool metal. I maneuvered the rope against the sharpest edge, sawing slowly back and forth.

Come on, come on, I urged silently. The rope fibers frayed little by little until, after an eternity, finally they split apart. My wrists came free!

Quickly I untied my legs and raced over to free Jenna.

She threw her arms around me when released, sobbing in relief.

"Thank you. I can't believe you came for me."

I hugged her tight. "I said I'd never give up on you. Now let's get the hell out of here."

I led the way and we crept to the door. Thankfully, he hadn't locked it. I opened it slowly and peered out, saw no one. We slipped out, closed the door silently behind us, and moved swiftly through the dark hallways, searching for an exit.

Finally, we came to a door with a lighted Exit sign above it. Freedom! Just as we were about to open it, shouts echoed down the hall.

They'd discovered our escape. Jenna whimpered but I squeezed her hand, signaling for quiet. We shrank back into the shadows, holding our breath.

Heavy footsteps drew nearer … then passed by. We waited a beat before slipping out the door into blessed fresh air and open sky.

We ran then, feet pounding the earth, until we'd put a small hill between us and the place we'd been held. We both sank to the ground, breathing deeply of the fresh air, looking up into the dark night sky. I checked my wrist. According to my watch, it had been seven hours since I'd found Kiley in Placitas. Judging by the darkness of the sky, we were nowhere near the city anymore.

"Do you know where we are?" I asked Jenna, checking to be sure she was breathing all right.

She shook her head. "I didn't recognize that room."

I crawled back to the top of the small ridge we'd dropped from. Below, at least five hundred feet in the distance, I saw lights and vehicles. Two buildings—both brightly lit. The ranch!

"We're at Talbot's ranch," I whispered to Jenna. "It looks like they're launching a search for us."

I watched as two vehicles headed down the dirt road that led to the highway. Two others spread out over the property. One was headed right toward us.

Chapter 45

We needed a better hiding place. The bright spotlights on the front of the vehicle would pinpoint us easily.

"Stay low," I cautioned. "We need to keep moving downhill, see if we can spot a rock outcropping or a thicket of trees to hide in."

There was no way we could outrun these guys, even if they left their vehicle behind. If Jenna felt anything like I did, her legs were weak, her head was pounding from the effects of the drug, and our reaction times were really blurry. I grabbed her hand and stumbled down the hillside, thankful again for the full moon.

Ahead, I spotted a clump of cottonwood trees. I pointed and she took my message. We reached them a fraction of a second before the spotlight swept the area. We'd both dropped to the ground, and the light moved on past.

"Can you climb a tree?" I asked.

"I used to do it all the time."

"Me too. Think you can do it now?"

She nodded. "Let's go up."

We each chose a tree and scaled it, at least as far as the lowest branch. Huffing a little, I managed to make it to the next branch up, into the leafier part of the tree, where I felt better concealed. Jenna moved a little slower, but she was in good shape and found herself a good hiding place as well.

From this vantage point we could see the two vehicles meandering through the high desert. The other two had returned, obviously not spotting us along the road to the highway.

Now what?

"Better get comfy. Looks like we'll have to sit it out until they give up," Jenna said.

Or until they came back, full force, with more lights and weapons. But I didn't say it. We settled in, getting as comfortable as it's possible to be in a tree.

I must have dozed, although it's hard to believe. My tailbone was aching something fierce and my fingers and toes were numb from the cold. When I opened my eyes and looked toward the ranch house again, I was astonished to see a veritable light show of red and blue.

"Jenna! Look!" I whispered. "The law has showed up."

It must be nearing six a.m. by now. The sky was lightening. A new day, one of hope and promise.

"Kiley!" She almost shouted her daughter's name, and I had to shush her.

"Did you see her?" The distance was too great, I felt sure. But I also felt sure that if Talbot had brought Kiley to the house, this would be our chance to find her and reunite mother and daughter—finally.

Jenna had climbed down and dropped stiffly to the ground, rubbing some warmth into her hands. I did the same, grabbing her arm just as she was about to take off running toward the melee below.

"Hold up. We don't know what's going on down there, and I don't want you running right back into a hostage situation or getting shot at."

It wasn't easy selling her on the idea of letting the events unfold. She was clearly desperate to find her daughter and hold her, but I persuaded her to climb to the top of the little hill and take a look first. Then the next small ridge, and the next clump of trees, making our way closer without giving away our presence.

As the coming sunrise revealed more, I recognized a familiar figure. Among the helmeted and vest-wearing ATF and Federal agents, tall and slim Alan Woodson was just walking away from the large metal building where I'd spotted the delivery truck a couple weeks ago now.

"C'mon, Jenna!" I ran toward him, that is until an armed agent in full gear aimed his weapon at me. That stopped me in my tracks and I raised my hands. Jenna pulled up short, right beside me.

Before I could attempt an explanation, Alan spotted me. "Charlie? Oh, thank goodness." He walked over and assured the ATF man we were all right. "Do you know how worried everyone is? Ron's been about to bite my head off, for two hours now."

"Um, yeah. I imagine so." Lesson to me: never expect that just because you started out on an adventure with a phone, a GPS, and a pistol, you'll end up with them at the end of the day. Or, the beginning of the next day. "I guess you'd better call him. I'll explain."

I'd actually left Drake a text with the address of the safehouse in Placitas where I was hoping to rescue Kiley and be home before bedtime, but that was another of those 'best laid plans' gone awry.

While I spoke with my brother, Jenna was quizzing Alan. I got about half of it (during the parts when Ron was chewing my rear in a nonstop barrage). Alan assured her the first thing they'd done when arriving at the location, after cuffing Talbot's security forces, was to ascertain that Talbot himself was not present. Then they performed a room-by-room search and located Kiley's belongings in a bedroom that appeared to be her own. "One of the security men told us she'd left with her dad."

"I need to see her," Jenna insisted.

"I can't let you head off to confront him yourself," Alan said. "We have to approach him with all due caution. With what we've got here and the other evidence we've collected, we believe we're dealing with a dangerous and well-armed man. But we have a plan."

That answer didn't sit well, but Jenna couldn't exactly argue with what he said.

Chapter 46

The next morning, Jenna took a deep breath as she stepped into the marble lobby at the courthouse, the click of her heels echoing off the walls. She'd borrowed a smart dress from Adrienne, a fitted sheath in a deep shade of eggplant, and the shoes to match. She turned to Adrienne, reaching out for a reassuring hand.

"Is it just me? This place feels heavy, oppressive, and yet cold and sterile at the same time." She rubbed her bare arms and adjusted her purse strap over her shoulder.

"You're just nervous, sweetie. Don't worry. They say the arraignment only takes a few minutes."

They walked together down the long corridor toward the courtroom, Jenna's pulse quickening with each step. She could almost feel Talbot's presence, smell his expensive cologne in the air.

Turning the corner, she froze. There he was, surrounded
by his high-priced lawyers, their expensive shoes shining,
cufflinks glinting in the harsh fluorescent lights.

Talbot looked up, his ice blue eyes meeting hers, and
smiled that predatory grin that still haunted her nightmares.
Jenna's stomach twisted. She wanted to run, to hide from
those searching eyes that stripped her bare. But she stood
firm, clenching her fists so tight her nails dug into her
palms, as her husband and his attorneys walked into the
courtroom.

Charlie and Ron walked up, and the Major Crimes
detective, Alan Woodson, was right behind them.

"How are you doing?" Charlie asked, compassion all
over her features.

Jenna tried for a brave smile, and wasn't sure she
succeeded.

"Where's Kiley?" she asked.

Yesterday had become a blur, once she and Charlie
left the ranch. Back to Adrienne's house for a shower and
fresh clothing, waiting for the phone to ring. She knew the
authorities were raiding the mansion, taking Talbot into
custody, but it was hell, wondering how it was going and
what was happening to her daughter.

Alan Woodson spoke up. "Your daughter is with her
grandparents. She's fine. When we arrived at Talbot's home
yesterday afternoon, we had already arranged with Grace
Farber to get there ahead of us. She was to find Kiley, get
her safely out the back door and to her own vehicle before
we approached Talbot. There's no way we were going to
let him use Kiley as a pawn, to put her in danger to save
his own skin."

"How did it go?" Charlie asked.

"Surprisingly easy. Talbot met us at the front door with

a smile, pretending it was simply an ordinary day, curious why we were there." Woodson rolled his eyes a little. "He feigned surprise when we announced he was under arrest and read the charges. His whole attitude was a joke. His attorneys were already there, seated in the living room, and they followed us downtown for the booking."

"Let me guess," Ron said. "Talbot was back home in time for dinner."

"Right."

"What will happen today?" Jenna asked, her voice a little shaky.

"The arraignment is a short proceeding where the charges will be read, and then he must state to the court whether he pleads guilty or not guilty. He'll plead not guilty, of course, and then his attorneys will probably take him out to breakfast."

"He won't be in jail?" Jenna asked.

Woodson shook his head. "Most likely not. We've stripped his power. Bank accounts are frozen, padlocks are on the gates and doors at the ranch property, his incoming mail at the mail drop is being confiscated, and his passport was already taken. He'll be under orders not to leave the county, and his lawyers will probably make him see that it would be a foolish move to try anything. If he breaks any of the court rules, he could be jailed instantly."

Jenna took a ragged breath. Everything he said should reassure her, but it wouldn't stop Talbot from harassing her or trying to keep Kiley. She put those thoughts aside and stood taller as the bailiff stepped out to let them know it was time for their case.

Chin up, Jenna strode into the courtroom, ready to face her demon at last. She sat rigidly on the hard wooden bench, back straight, eyes fixed ahead. She could feel Talbot's gaze when he turned around, willing her to acknowledge him. But she resisted, jaw clenched, breathing measured. Adrienne sat on one side of her, Charlie on the other. Ron sat by Charlie, staring daggers at their former client.

The bailiff called the court to order. The judge entered, a short blonde woman with black robes swishing. As the charges were read, Jenna's pulse thundered in her ears.

"How do you plead?" the judge asked in a bored tone.

"Not guilty, Your Honor," came Talbot's coached reply.

The judge read some instructions, basically informing Talbot of the same things Woodson had just told the group outside in the hall, that he was not to leave the county and if he did so, his bail would be revoked and he would be brought into custody. She banged her gavel and called for the next case.

Talbot and his attorneys rose, cleared their things, and passed through the bar into the gallery area. Jenna's nails dug into her thighs. Of course he would deny everything, continue to spin his side of the story to make himself look innocent. She refused to look at him as he walked past.

"Let's go," Ron said, turning to the little group. "We've got more important things to do than think about that jerk."

They stood, the four of them, and walked out to the corridor.

When she saw Talbot, smiling as if he'd just shared a joke with his attorneys, she couldn't hold back any longer. "You monster!" Jenna burst out.

All eyes turned to her. She trembled but met Talbot's icy stare.

"All these years … you made her believe I abandoned her. My own daughter!" Jenna's voice broke.

Talbot just gazed at her calmly. "I told Kiley the truth, my dear. That you must have perished at sea. You surely would have come back if you'd loved her."

Jenna shook with rage. "You know that's a lie! You left me there to die!"

Talbot gave her a pitying look. "Such delusions," he murmured, just loud enough for her to hear. "Don't worry, I'll take good care of Kiley."

Charlie stepped forward and took Jenna's arm. "Don't engage with him," she muttered under her breath. "Seeing you become rattled is exactly what he wants. He won't get custody of Kiley. Not after all this."

Jenna clenched her jaw, glaring back. She wouldn't let him twist the truth, not this time. Her nightmare was ending. She took a deep breath, trying to calm her pounding heart as the past flooded back.

She had been so naive, so trusting of Talbot. He had swept her off her feet with his charm and lavish gifts. But each time she had threatened to leave him, to take their daughter and go, his cool confidence disarmed her. He always said, "No one leaves me, Jenna. And no one will ever take Kiley from me."

And so she'd made her plan, plunging into the dark water, the black waves closing over her head. Swimming for her life, with her meager documentation to see her into a new life. And Talbot had been content to leave her for dead.

Jenna snapped back to the present. She had to be strong, to fight back. For her daughter and for herself. She would not let him silence her again.

"I know what you did," Jenna said, her voice low but steady. "And I'll make sure everyone knows the truth."

Talbot's eyes narrowed almost imperceptibly. Then he smiled. "No one will believe you, my dear. It's your word against mine. And we both know how this will end."

Jenna held his icy gaze, refusing to look away. But then she felt her resolve wavering under Talbot's calm stare. He had always been able to make her feel small, insignificant. Even now, after everything she had survived, he still had that power.

She dug her fingernails into her palms, using the pain to center herself. "I gathered proof," she said, desperation creeping into her voice. "I—I kept records, documents …"

Charlie nudged her, warning her not to say too much.

Talbot laughed then, the sound sending a chill down Jenna's spine. "Come now, we both know that's not true. Anything you kept, from years ago, will be hopelessly outdated now." He leaned in, his voice dangerous. "You have nothing on me. No one will believe your wild stories over the word of an upstanding businessman."

Jenna recoiled, wavering.

"Talbot …" one of the slick attorneys said, tapping his client's arm, pointing toward the exit doors.

He spun, as if leaving had been his idea, and the three men walked out of the building.

Jenna felt her legs weaken. She longed to embrace Kiley, to feel her daughter's arms around her again. She could not let this evil man win. Ron stepped forward and placed a steadying hand on her elbow.

Jenna blinked back tears, knowing the most difficult part was yet to come. But she would find a way to make Kiley understand the truth. She had to believe that.

For now, all she could do was walk away, carrying the weight of Talbot's silent smirk with her.

Jenna walked out of the courthouse in a daze, barely registering the reporters calling her name or the cameras flashing in her face. She felt Ron's steadying hand on her back as he guided her down the courthouse steps, but inside she was crumbling.

Once in the safety of Adrienne's car, the tears came in earnest. She wept for the years lost with Kiley, for the web of lies Talbot had spun about her. Adrienne said nothing, just drove in silence.

When her sobs finally subsided, Jenna raised her head. "I can't let him get away with this," she said, her voice raw but firm.

"Trust the process, sweetie. His fancy lawyers can't hide the truth forever. You heard Detective Woodson— they've got a ton of evidence against him. Thanks to you."

Jenna wiped her eyes, grasping onto that slim thread of hope. Talbot wasn't behind bars yet, but the case was far from over.

And now, she was ready to meet her grown daughter.

Chapter 47

I'd spoken with Grace Farber this morning, discussing a plan for the mother-daughter reunion. Even Jenna had agreed that the courthouse was too public and it would not be good for Kiley to see her father as a defendant, perhaps even being ordered to jail, if that's how the proceeding had gone.

As it turned out, I was thankful she hadn't seen her mom's emotional outburst or the nasty way in which Talbot had put her down. Ron and I were in his car, leading the way for Adrienne and Jenna to follow to my house. This is a new thing for me—my home is normally my sacred space and I've rarely invited a client here. Grace had offered their home for the meeting, but there were too many unknowns. For one, Talbot could show up.

This seemed like the right mix, out of the public eye,

out of Talbot's grasp, and a place that held no emotional ties for the parties involved. Plus, Drake had offered to stay home while the rest of us went to court. He would have coffee and pastries ready, in case anyone had an appetite.

I'd already phoned Grace, the moment the court proceeding ended. She and Mitch and Kiley would be waiting for us. I found myself getting a butterfly or two as we made the turn onto my street. Stately old elms leafing out, blue spruce, and flowering plum trees reminded me that we had a lovely spring day for the occasion. Meanwhile, I hoped the Farbers had been able to overcome Talbot's snide indoctrination, the lies he'd been feeding Kiley for most of her life.

As we pulled into the driveway, the front door opened. I felt myself holding my breath. Adrienne parked in front of the house and I saw Jenna fiddling with her seatbelt. When she opened her door and looked toward the house, her eyes widened. She made it across our front lawn in a flash.

Kiley didn't hesitate at all. They met in an embrace that made my throat contract and my eyes prickle with tears.

I could hear Jenna murmuring, "It's okay, baby. It's all going to be okay," over and over again.

Ron and I joined up with Adrienne, whose eyes were streaming at the sight. We held back, giving the pair their moment.

* * *

Fifteen minutes later, we'd all settled inside the house. Drake met everyone and then quietly disappeared into his office. Jenna wrapped her hands around the warm mug he'd given her, the scent of dark roast coffee wafting up. Next to her on the sofa, Kiley brushed a lock of hair behind her ear, sitting a little sideways and not taking her eyes off her mother.

"I can't believe it's really you," Kiley said, eyes shining. "After all these years of thinking you were gone, and now here you are."

Jenna beamed. "You look so much like I did at your age."

"Tell me about Alaska. Is it cold? Do you have dogsleds and igloos?"

With a soft laugh, Jenna launched into descriptions of the glacial beauty of Alaska—the jagged mountains, the crystalline lakes, the nights when the northern lights danced across the sky.

Kiley listened, captivated. Back in that safehouse, when I'd found her, Kiley seemed skeptical that we'd found Jenna, alive and well. I was glad Grace had stepped in to talk to her, to verify what we were saying. There was so much to catch up on, so many lost years to account for. But for now, it was enough to sit together on a bright spring day.

Jenna trailed off, her gaze dropping to the coffee mug clutched between her hands. She took a shaky breath.

"There's something I need to tell you," she said quietly. "The reason I disappeared … it wasn't by choice."

Kiley furrowed her brow, leaning forward. "What do you mean?"

Jenna's knuckles whitened around the ceramic mug. "You're going to learn that your father … he's been involved in some dangerous things. Illegal things." She looked up, eyes glistening. "I overheard a conversation while we were aboard the cruise ship. Bad people were after us. They were planning to come after me. I had no choice but to get away." She cleared her throat, searching for words. "I had a plan, initially, to come back for you so we could escape together."

"Dad?" Kiley whispered in disbelief. "But he just sells cars ..."

"That's only his public face." Jenna's voice shook. "There's worse. Much worse. And I want you to be ready for things you might hear on the news or from other people when his trial starts."

Kiley stood up and paced the length of the room, her mouth falling open. "This can't be real. He's strict, sometimes has a temper, but he's always been caring in his own way—he's mixed up in crimes? It doesn't make sense."

Jenna wiped hastily at a tear. "My original plan was to take you with me, but Talbot foiled it. Once I went over the rail on that ship, I hoped your grandparents would take care of you. That you'd have a good, safe life until I could come for you. I even had a passport made for you in another name." She reached for her daughter, grasping Kiley's hand as she walked by. "I'm so sorry it didn't go the way I planned."

Kiley stared at her mother, clearly stunned. She gave Jenna's hand a squeeze, holding on like a lifeline.

"Tell me everything," she whispered.

I fidgeted with my coffee mug. "We should leave you—"

Jenna took a shaky breath, keeping her eyes locked on Kiley's. "I'd like for our friends to hear this, if you don't mind."

Kiley looked up, nodding toward each of us in turn. "Yes, please stay. I have the feeling you all know most of this already."

I lowered myself to a chair. Adrienne stood beside Jenna, rubbing the back of her friend's neck.

"I don't know …" Jenna said. "A lot of it isn't appropriate for—"

"Everything!" Kiley insisted. "You said I was probably going to hear it on the news anyway."

Jenna took a deep breath. "It started years ago, before you were born. Your father always wanted more money, more success. From the car business, he started doing side deals, starting with making high-interest loans to desperate people who can't pay on time, scaring them. Some of his referrals come from casino bosses, who know the gambling addicts. Eventually he moved on to money laundering." She glanced up at Grace and Mitch. "I didn't know how deep it went at first, whether you were aware."

Both of the older Farbers shook their heads, Mitch appearing dumbfounded.

Jenna continued, "Then the late-night meetings started. Strange men coming and going from the house. That was when I first began to get an inkling."

She paused, taking a sip of coffee. "One night, Kiley, when you were about two years old, I overheard something I shouldn't have. An argument about a botched job, threats of retaliation. I realized this was serious stuff."

Kiley squeezed her eyes shut, obviously trying to reconcile this story with the father who had raised her. I could practically read her thoughts. Stern, yes. Controlling, even cold at times. But a criminal mastermind?

"Things escalated quickly after that. His temper with me, his stress over his business deals," Jenna continued, voice stronger now. "When I realized I was almost never left alone, I started making plans, and I knew the only way to protect myself—and you—was to disappear. To escape somehow and start over somewhere far away, with a new name."

She gave a bitter laugh. "Your father always liked to be in control. But I took that away from him. I left on my terms."

Kiley opened her eyes, seeing the determination in her mother's face. Understanding washed over her.

"You were so brave," she said softly. "I can't imagine how hard it was for you."

Jenna's eyes filled with fresh tears. "My only regret was leaving you. But I didn't have a choice. Once I realized I couldn't simply come back for you, at least I knew Grace and Mitch would step in and raise you right."

Kiley moved around the table, wrapping her mother in a fierce hug. "You did what you had to," she murmured. "I'm just glad I have you again."

They held each other close, tears flowing freely. Jenna pulled back first, dabbing at her eyes with a napkin. She shook her head in disgust. "I was *so* naive when we first married. Too blinded by the fancy cars and big house to see the truth. By the time I figured it out, it was too late."

Kiley stared into empty space. "I grew up with such a lavish lifestyle. The private schools, luxury vacations, my pony when I was ten, the infinity pool in the back yard. A little embarrassing at times, for my friends to see all that. Was it all bought with dirty money?"

Jenna gave a shrug. "Probably not all of it. The dealerships were the legitimate front for the rest."

"Why didn't you go to the police?" she asked. "They could have protected you."

Jenna let out a bitter laugh. "Oh, Kiley. Your father has connections everywhere, even in law enforcement. I had no one I could trust. Even now, I'm nervous that someone in power will override the honest officers we've met and could still get him off the hook."

She reached across the table and squeezed Kiley's hand.

"I'm just so thankful you have your grandparents. At least I knew you'd be cared for and kept away from all of … his business deals."

Kiley blinked back fresh tears, giving her grandparents a grateful smile. "I'm so sorry, Mom," she said, "I had no idea what you went through."

"None of us did," Grace added, regret showing on her face.

Jenna stroked Kiley's hair, just like she used to when Kiley was small. "It's okay, sweetie. None of it was your fault."

"I want to help you," Kiley said. "For everything Dad put you through. Whatever you need, I'm here."

Jenna smiled, though her eyes were wary. "I appreciate that, but this could get dangerous."

Kiley lifted her chin. "I don't care. He doesn't scare me."

Jenna regarded her daughter—so grown up yet still so young. "Seriously, honey. The law will take over now. We've now got some trustworthy people working on it who are beyond his reach."

Kiley smiled tentatively.

Jenna glanced around the assembled group. "But for now, let's keep this among us. I don't want anyone finding out I'm back in town until I have a better handle on the situation, until I know friend from foe."

Kiley nodded. "I won't tell a soul."

Grace Farber exchanged a look with her husband.

Connie Shelton

Then she spoke up. "You know, you two don't have to stay in Albuquerque."

"What we mean is," Mitch added, "we'd miss you like crazy, baby, but if there's a safer place …"

"At least until the trial is over and the rest of those bad people are flushed out," Grace said.

Ron and I straightened up. "You know … that's not a bad idea," he said.

Kiley looked at her mother. Jenna smiled, the most genuine one I'd seen yet. "So … what should we do now? We can go anywhere, do anything we want."

Kiley considered. "Anywhere would be better than here. Let's go far away and start over. Just you and me."

Jenna smiled, picturing it. "A quaint cottage by the ocean, or a cozy cabin in the mountains. I suppose it doesn't really matter, as long as we're together."

For the first time since Talbot Farber had walked into our office, I felt a sense of rightness.

Chapter 48

The next morning Jenna woke with the unreal feeling that she was finally free. Kiley slept soundly in the matching twin bed in Adrienne's guest room. Jenna felt a welling of love for this daughter she hardly knew.

Immediately after the reunion at Charlie's house, the elder Farbers had gone to Talbot's huge house to pack Kiley's things. Interestingly, when asked for a list of what to bring, Kiley had only asked for a few clothes, the contents of her bookshelf, and the old photos of her mother and herself together. Well aware of the limitations of Jenna's little sedan, they'd packed those items accordingly.

Jenna dressed in the bathroom and quietly tiptoed from the bedroom, joining Adrienne at the kitchen counter, accepting the mug of coffee her friend offered.

"Wow, what a day that was," Adrienne said. Yesterday

had been such a turbulent whirlwind of emotion, they'd all fallen asleep early.

Jenna nodded. Life had changed so much in the past week. She could hardly keep up.

"So … where do you think you'll go?"

"We're heading north. At this point, that's all I know. A day at a time, as they say."

"You going to be okay, moneywise? I have some savings."

"Which you will not give away," Jenna said. "We're okay. The Farbers get a pretty hefty partner share from the dealerships. They'd already set up a trust fund for Kiley. Mitch is doing the paperwork this morning to change the trustee from Talbot to me. He said the minute this whole thing came crashing down, he was going to do that anyway. The poor man has lost all faith in his son, sad to say."

A knock sounded at the door and Adrienne hurried to find out who it was.

"Charlie! Come in for coffee."

Jenna turned to see her newest friend walk in, a bakery box in her hands.

"We had stuff left from yesterday. It seems everyone was way more into talking than eating." Charlie grinned and set the box on the counter, then accepted a coffee.

Shuffling footsteps sounded in the hallway and Kiley appeared, yawning, her blonde hair in a tangle. She opted for hot chocolate instead of coffee, reminding Jenna that this was still her little girl.

"So, you two are on the road today," Charlie said. "I thought maybe I could help you pack."

"There's not a whole lot," Jenna admitted. "I had one suitcase when I left Alaska, and Kiley is even going minimalist right now."

Kiley came up and rested her head on her shoulder.

"No regrets, right Mom?"

Jenna turned to her daughter, her reason for living. "No regrets at all."

"I don't expect you to reveal your plans—maybe you haven't even made them," Charlie said, "but please keep in touch. We want to know you're doing all right."

"Yeah … about that." Jenna's face grew serious for a moment. "Being that I still don't know the extent of Talbot's outlaw network, we're using our alternate IDs. If you get a note from Nancy Miller or Katie Miller … well, you'll know."

She stood up and poured herself more coffee from the carafe. "I may be forced to come back and testify at the trial. Not looking forward to that—at all. But Adrienne has put me in touch with a good attorney, someone Talbot doesn't know, from Santa Fe."

"A client of mine," her friend said with a little flourish.

"He's advised me to not speak until spoken to, basically. If I'm needed to help prove the prosecution's case, they'll get word to me. But hopefully the evidence they gathered is enough to make it a slam-dunk, without my being there." She turned to Kiley. "Well, you'd better get dressed, kiddo. The car is leaving here in twenty minutes."

Charlie walked out with them, carrying a tote bag. "Please be careful. For sure, until you're out of New Mexico, don't trust anyone." She paused a moment. "Actually, knowing Talbot was connected in Washington, DC and other places … just watch your backs."

"Oh, I'm very accustomed to that," Jenna assured her as Kiley walked out of the house.

They climbed into the car, both giddy with excitement about the unknown adventure ahead. As Jenna drove north on I-25, she glanced in the rearview mirror, watching the city grow smaller and smaller until it disappeared from view.

"Goodbye Talbot," she whispered. A weight seemed to lift from her chest.

* * *

The first few hours of the drive were filled with lively conversation and laughter, as they brainstormed ideas for their new home and lives. They bypassed Denver, keeping to the less-traveled highways, debating between a small town or big city for their destination. Near the ocean, somewhere with desert views, or up in the mountains? The possibilities were endless.

As night fell, Kiley drifted off to sleep. Jenna continued driving through the darkness, fueled by caffeine and anticipation. The road seemed to stretch on forever as they entered Wyoming, but she didn't mind. Each mile brought them closer to freedom.

Finally, just before midnight, Jenna saw a sign: "Welcome to Pine Valley." She gently shook Kiley awake. "What do you think?"

Kiley's eyes fluttered open and she sat up with a smile, taking in the trees and the rustic cabin homes. "I love it!"

Jenna pulled into the parking lot of a small motel on the edge of town. "This will be a great place to start, anyway." She and Kiley grabbed their bags from the trunk and headed to the front office.

The clerk, an elderly man with kind eyes, greeted them warmly. "Welcome to Pine Valley. Just passing through?"

"Actually, we're looking to rent one of your rooms for a little while," Jenna said.

The man nodded. "We have a nice unit available.

Furnished too, with a kitchenette."

Jenna did some quick math in her head. The money she had withdrawn would easily cover a month or two here. And she could pick up work waitressing or cleaning houses. She didn't plan to touch Kiley's trust fund—that was for college. Meanwhile, this could work.

"We'll take it," she said decisively.

Kiley gave her mom's hand a squeeze, pride shining in her eyes. Jenna had done it—found them a safe new home. The motel room was small but cozy. Jenna sat on one of the twin beds, suddenly overcome with emotion. The tears came without warning.

Kiley sat next to her. "It's going to be okay, Mom. We're together now. That's all that matters."

Jenna wiped her eyes and took a deep breath. "I'm sorry, sweetie. It's just … everything we've been through to get here. I keep thinking how naive I was, throughout all of this."

Kiley squeezed her mom's hand. "You don't have to apologize. I can't even imagine what it was like being married to him."

Jenna nodded slowly. "At first it felt like a dream come true. Even when the façade began to crack—the glimpses of his temper, his need for control—I made excuses. I thought I could change him."

Kiley listened quietly, her heart aching for her mother.

Jenna looked into her daughter's eyes. "You were the one good thing to come from that nightmare of a relationship. My ray of light. From the moment I held you, I knew I'd do anything to protect you."

Kiley hugged her mom tightly. "You did protect me. You're so strong, Mom. We have a fresh start now. We're free."

Chapter 49

I sank into the worn leather chair in Ron's office, letting out a weary sigh. Ron sat across from me, looking equally exhausted. It was way after hours, and I still hadn't caught up on my normal duties after traveling and bringing Jenna Farber home, with everything that entailed.

"Well, that was one heck of a case," I said.

Ron nodded. "No kidding. I'm glad we were able to bring that jerk to justice. I heard on the news that Senator Gallegos is being questioned. Of course, the report was pretty vague."

I shrugged, wondering how high in state politics this game would eventually go. "I'll need your time sheets, the expense records. We're going to bill the Farber corporations for every penny of this agony."

We sat in silence for a moment, reflecting. The missing

persons report, routine interviews, paper trails, and phone records. But it had quickly spiraled into something much darker—the offshore accounts, the weapons, and worst of all, the way he treated his family.

Ron's thoughts followed mine. "Like they were possessions. Objects to control."

"It's scary to think how easily a monster can hide behind a friendly and businesslike façade, isn't it?" I thought back to Jenna, half-conscious, drugged, when I found her at the ranch. The narrow escape, the hours we sat, freezing our butts off in those trees, terrified we'd be caught.

"I'm so grateful we were able to get Jenna and Kiley together. And they're free of him now," I said.

Ron nodded. "Have you heard anything?"

I shook my head. And then my phone pinged with a text message. I picked it out of my pocket and took a look. A photo of a roadside sign. "Welcome to Pine Valley," I read. "Any idea where that is?"

"Never heard of it."

"Good. Let's hope Talbot hasn't either."

He reached into his desk drawer and pulled out a bottle of Glenlivet 12, holding it up with a question in his eyes. "Celebrate?"

I nodded. Why not? What had started as a simple missing person case had ended up cracking a fairly major crime ring, and we could be proud of our part. I accepted the glass he handed me, and we clinked them together. I winced a little at the bite of the Scotch—I'm normally more of a one-glass-of-wine girl.

I pictured the little cabin in Alaska where I'd finally caught up with Jenna. In a rustic sort of way, she'd seemed content there. Maybe that's where she and Kiley would end up. With her daughter, I could see Jenna happy in that lifestyle.

I had no idea what the future would hold for them. They didn't either, most likely. But for certain, if one of her future texts included a photo of a cabin and a pile of firewood … well, I'd never reveal its location.

Thank you for taking the time to read *Cruises Can Be Murder*. If you enjoyed it, please consider telling your friends or posting a short review. Word of mouth is an author's best friend and is much appreciated.

Thank you,
Connie

* * *

As always, a huge thanks goes out to my editor, Stephanie Dewey, and my beta reader team: Marcia Koopmann, Susan Gross, Sandra Anderson, Isobel Tamney, and Paula Webb. Every book benefits from your expertise and sharp eyes on my manuscripts. Thank you, thank you, thank you! And, of course, my undying thanks goes out to you—my readers. Your support over the years means everything to me.

* * *

Sign up for Connie Shelton's free mystery newsletter at www.connieshelton.com and receive advance information about new books, along with a chance at prizes, discounts and other mystery news!

Contact by email: connie@connieshelton.com
Follow Connie Shelton on Twitter, Pinterest, Instagram and Facebook

Books by Connie Shelton

The Charlie Parker Series
Deadly Gamble
Vacations Can Be Murder
Partnerships Can Be Murder
Small Towns Can Be Murder
Memories Can Be Murder
Honeymoons Can Be Murder
Reunions Can Be Murder
Competition Can Be Murder
Balloons Can Be Murder
Obsessions Can Be Murder
Gossip Can Be Murder
Stardom Can Be Murder
Phantoms Can Be Murder
Buried Secrets Can Be Murder
Legends Can Be Murder
Weddings Can Be Murder
Alibis Can Be Murder
Escapes Can Be Murder
Old Bones Can Be Murder
Sweethearts Can Be Murder
Money Can Be Murder
Road Trips Can Be Murder
Cruises Can Be Murder
Holidays Can Be Murder - a Christmas novella

Children's Books
Daisy and Maisie and the Great Lizard Hunt
Daisy and Maisie and the Lost Kitten

The Samantha Sweet Series

Sweet Masterpiece
Sweet's Sweets
Sweet Holidays
Sweet Hearts
Bitter Sweet
Sweets Galore
Sweets Begorra
Sweet Payback
Sweet Somethings
Sweets Forgotten
Spooky Sweet
Sticky Sweet
Sweet Magic
Deadly Sweet Dreams
The Ghost of Christmas Sweet
Tricky Sweet
Haunted Sweets
Spellbound Sweets – a Halloween novella
The Woodcarver's Secret – the series prequel

The Heist Ladies Series

Diamonds Aren't Forever
The Trophy Wife Exchange
Movie Mogul Mama
Homeless in Heaven
Show Me the Money

Milton Keynes UK
Ingram Content Group UK Ltd.
UKHW010635040324
438885UK00001B/31